Madeline • Samuel • Evelyn

## Acknowledgements

Scripture quotations are taken from the Holy Bible, New Living
Translation, copyright ©1996, 2004, 2015 by Tyndale House Foundation.
Used by permission of Tyndale House Publishers, Inc., Carol Stream,
Illinois 60188. All rights reserved.

Illustrated by Dawn Southcombe (Dawnie-chan)
Design & Typography by Tim Roberts (Fatcalf.co.uk)

Thank you to St Peter's Saltley Trust for providing funding and support at
the early stages of the project - particularly to enable the commissioning
of the illustrations which form such an important part of this book and
the accompanying schools workshop.

Early development thanks: Liz Swan, Kim Wigley, Sam Philips, Louise
Prockter, Samuel Prockter, Madeline Prockter, Solly Williams, Jon Stark,
and Lucy Southcombe.

# ACT I

# LEGEND OF THE KEY

## CHAPTER ONE

# NINGEN

"I magine what it would be like if the things you feel could turn into real places?

"Don't get too carried away; it's not as great as it might sound.

"Yeah, Happiness is a great place. I've been there.

"The problem is, it doesn't last long. And once you leave, it's so hard to get back.

"My name's Ningen, by the way.

"As in Nin-gen.

"It's a weird name, I know.

"It sort of matches the situation we're in now. Not my name, I mean – but how weird things are at the moment.

"Not that things were ever not. Strange, I mean. But yeah, I'm in a real mess.

"That's why I'm so pleased to talk to you right now.

"Anyway, this is what Kana told me. I might tell you more about her later, because she was fantastic. You'd have loved her! She's gone now, but she used to say, 'Be careful; even though happiness is a place you want to live, there are other places you need to be careful not to get trapped in.'

"Kana and I loved to play together, but there were times she got really serious. She'd say, 'Imagine a lie: it's not just that you feel alone when you're hiding something; you could easily get trapped inside it and cut off from everyone.'

"I asked her what that place was like, but all she said was that it was a wilderness; a desert.

"There are worse places to get stuck though, you know. The ice plains sound horrible; that's where you go when hate takes you over. Then there's stone. There's no coming back from there. Not for me, anyway.

"One time, Kana looked me right in the eyes, her face creased in a frown, and she told me something I wish I'd taken more seriously at the time. 'If we ever get split up, if you ever get trapped, you'll never see me again.'

"Do you know, I was beginning to think there wasn't anyone else in the entire world. It sounds silly to say now, cos here you are, but… okay. I'm going to tell you something personal, but you've got to keep it to yourself.

"I wasn't born.

"Well, I was born, but I wasn't a baby.

"I was made!

"I was made fully grown.

"A bit like you, actually.

"Well, not exactly, but close enough.

"I used to dream about other people like you. I even dreamt about a king one time.

"It was so real.

"The king was on a white horse, and I followed him through a forest. These warriors were surrounding him, and there were hundreds of fantastic creatures. It was incredible… but then the dream went wrong. It turned into a nightmare. Another man came to fight the king. He was scary, dark wings sprouting from his back, and he wielded two swords as he blasted through the air. He attacked the king with these crazy animals fighting for him, and as I watched, I got carried away by the branches of the tree I live under today. Sounds crazy, I know.

"Wow, has anyone ever told you how easy you are to talk to? Listen to me going on!"

Ningen paused for a moment and frowned to himself.

"Anyway… I bet you'd love it if I kept telling you my secrets, wouldn't you? Shame, really; I'd quite like to, but the sun is far too hot for me to be standing in." He looked to the sky, shielding his eyes with a very sandy arm. "Yeah, I need to get home."

He took a moment to wipe the sweat from his brow. The heat was impossible, and the sand from the desert wilderness got everywhere. Generally speaking, Ningen wouldn't venture this far away from his cave home under the only shade in the area. But needs must, and he had not found himself in this kind of situation before.

He crouched down closer to the person he'd been speaking to. He'd dug a hole earlier in the day and shoved him into it. He had no real plan, but this seemed like the safest way to protect himself from the intruder.

"It's odd," Ningen said to the stranger. "You look a lot like the warriors from my dream. Same face, same armour…" He leant in a little further and grabbed roughly at the man's back. "Same wings."

If he were to be honest, Ningen felt quite afraid. But he tried hard not to let it show, even trying to sound calm and friendly as he manhandled the stranger in the sandy pit. "I'm sorry, my friend, you're going to have to stay here for now."

The warrior looked up and made a slight breathy noise, gesturing as if he wanted to speak. But Ningen interrupted. "Save your strength. Who knows, maybe if you concentrate, you might be able to will yourself to a happier place. It's not worked for me yet, but…" he shrugged, "…you never know."

And with that, Ningen patted the warrior on the cheek, got up, brushed the sand off himself, and made his way back to his cave home, obsessing the entire way about how he'd ended up in this position in the first place.

Of course, this was a horrible place to live, but it hadn't always been this way. In the beginning, it was just about as perfect as anything could be. A place of pure joy.

## CHAPTER TWO

# HAPPINESS

The relationship between Kana and Ningen was incredibly special, and they loved to play together in the woods around the clearing. Each morning Ningen awoke to a feast Kana had laid out for them, and he and Kana enjoyed it together. Although he was created as a grown man, his mind was young and innocent like a child's. He enjoyed his time with Kana and was always excited about the next thing they would do together.

One evening, as Kana settled Ningen down for sleep, the stars swirling above them, she told him the story of how he came to be.

"Kana, where do we come from?" he said.

"That's a difficult question to answer," said Kana, wondering how much he'd be able to understand. "Close your eyes and imagine the games we play in the woods."

Ningen squeezed his eyes as closed as they'd go, and Kana let out a little giggle at the sight. "Are you imagining?"

"Yes, I'm thinking hard – just tell the story already!"

"Okay. Imagine if every time we weaved between a tree, and laughed, and jumped over flowers, it made magic – like amazing colours and sounds springing from our feet as we played—"

"Whoa, that sounds amazing!" interrupted Ningen.

"Shhh! Listen, the best part's coming up," teased Kana. "Imagine if all of that magic could actually make everything you see around us."

Ningen was inspired. "Did we come from the magic of someone playing?"

Kana smiled. "Yes, in a way *you* did. Now head off to sleep; we'll have some more adventures in the morning."

"Where are you going, Kana?"

"Well. You know the grasslands already, where we live; I like to think of this as a place where I'm happiest. Well, there's an even better place. It's massive, like eternity. It's where I come from, and when you sleep and you're safely dreaming, I drift back there sometimes. But don't worry, you'll be safe here as I go and I'll be back ready to play in the morning."

"Can I go there?" Ningen couldn't really understand what she meant.

"One day," Kana replied, "but not today."

Ningen began to drift off to sleep, images from Kana's magical stories filling his mind. But when she moved away, he stirred and woke up with a start. "Kana? Can we play by the tree tomorrow?"

Kana knelt beside him and stroked his brow to settle him back down. "We can play over here, in the grasslands, and the woods, and we can explore. But we can't play by the tree. It isn't safe."

"Pleeease!" protested a very sleepy Ningen.

"It's too dangerous, sweetheart. The desert behind the tree is a place you can easily become trapped, and I can't go there. We can play anywhere but the tree, okay?"

As Ningen fell back off to sleep, Kana drifted away. A cool breeze swirled around Ningen as he turned over and snuggled himself up in the warm, soft grass surrounding him.

At the other end of the grasslands something stirred below the tree that dominated the landscape on the desert's edge. It was little wonder Ningen was desperate to play there, but Kana was right to worry. That tree was alive. It almost seemed to be waiting for him to want to visit. Its dark, winding roots pulsed with magic, and its branches reached towards Ningen, swaying in the breeze. They sensed his curiosity and began to call to him in his sleep.

Over the following week, Ningen and Kana settled into a routine that ended with a story each night, which gave Ningen a deeper feeling of awe and wonder for the world around him.

After a while, he started to feel more confident, and his curiosity about the other side of the grasslands increased. As he and Kana played, he could see there was something on the other side of the tree, and he was beginning to think Kana was afraid of it. Maybe if he could go over to check it out, he could show her it was okay.

One evening, Kana told him the story of creation again and, like a naughty child, he pretended to fall asleep. After she left, he got up and started to make his way towards the tree. If he was quick, he could get there and back before morning.

## CHAPTER THREE

# DISAPPOINTMENT

Ningen made his way across the field, creeping through a very dark, long shadow spreading all the way from the tree right back to the clearing where he was supposed to be asleep. The moon was far up in the sky, and an unfamiliar cold breeze made him shiver.

The long branches of the tree drew forward, reaching for Ningen as if trying to take hold of him. He swept them out of the way and looked around. It was far too dark, so he made his way around the back to where the moon was lighting up the desert in the distance. He climbed down the bank and swung around the thick roots before landing on the soft, cool sand with a hollow sounding thud.

A sweet smell wafted from the back of the tree – it seemed to be coming from the roots themselves. Ningen leaned in, grabbing a hanging root, and was amazed when he realised the warm, fragrant aroma was clinging to it. What a fantastic tree this was!

He climbed into the sprawling structure and snapped a slightly broken root. The strange substance inside was thick like treacle – it smelled sweet, and glowed with a soft warmth that drew Ningen in, bewitching his mind. He stripped off the outer layer and feasted on the root, devouring it as if he'd never eaten before.

Afterwards, Ningen gathered some wood to make a fire, and then warmed the tree's roots up in the burning embers. This was quite possibly the naughtiest thing he'd ever done, and his heart raced with the pure excitement of doing something in secret for the very first time. "This is the life," he thought. Fun, freedom, and a little danger to make things even more interesting.

Ningen remained very pleased with himself as he feasted for most of the night, until his stomach groaned with the sheer weight of it all. He was so full he couldn't get comfortable, and he spent what felt like ages doubled over with a stabbing pain in his gut. This was an amazing adventure, but if he were honest with himself the night was far too long, and he was beginning to long for morning. Finally, the sun began to rise, and he heaved his full belly back to the clearing to meet Kana for breakfast.

Kana was already waiting for him with a wonderful banquet of food for them to enjoy together. She smiled at him. "Good morning, Ningen! How did you sleep?"

Ningen had hardly slept a wink – he'd been too busy filling his face. Still, he wasn't going to share that with Kana. "I didn't sleep great, to be honest. How about you?"

"I don't really need much sleep, Ningen. I've been preparing this food for you. This is what I do while you sleep."

A pang of guilt churned in Ningen's stomach. He had never thought about all the things Kana did for him before. "That's great. Thank you so much, but… I'm not really hungry today. I feel a bit poorly."

Ningen had never had to lie before.

Kana knew precisely what he had been doing, but she played along and let him continue with his story.

"Yeah, I think I'll just go for a nap or something. Thanks for the food, though… maybe I could have some later?" He smiled awkwardly at Kana, gave her a quick kiss on the cheek, and made his way into the woods to lie down.

It took him ages to get off to sleep. The sounds from within the woods were keeping him alert, but it was his mind that stopped him from sleeping. His mind was racing with the events of the night before and, although the feeling of independence was exciting, the feeling he'd disappointed Kana overwhelmed him.

## CHAPTER FOUR

# DREAMS

Eventually, Ningen fell asleep, but for the first time in his life a nightmare captured his mind.

It began with the sensation of being too deep in water. Light and shadows raced past his eyes, but there was no air to breathe. Next, the unmistakable feeling of falling shook his entire body. Wind rushed past him, and something like fog dissolved into the sky above him. Next came a cold snap, followed immediately by a blazing fire. Within moments, Ningen was trapped in between two rocks, staring up at a sky that was breaking up while spewing fire and ice. He wanted to scream, but no sound came out. What a horrible dream this was, and so frightening.

His dreamscape shimmered and then changed as he found himself back in his resting place in the field, and he opened his eyes to look around. He was stunned by the beauty of the trees around him. The sound of the rustling leaves was like music, singing praise to someone called the *King of the Eternal Dimension*. Ningen had no idea who that was supposed to be, but he was captivated by the emotion of the song and got up to follow it to see where it might take him.

He walked through the woods, in awe at the sound of the singing and the colours encircling him. In the distance, a figure of blinding light rode confidently towards him on a white horse. The rider didn't acknowledge Ningen as he rode straight past him towards the clearing. He had wings of pure light, and in his hands sparks crackled like lightning. Ningen reached up to touch him, but his hand passed through horse and rider as though they were a cloud.

Ningen followed him into the clearing and then stood still, taken aback by the sight of several strange, winged creatures surrounding the man and his horse. In the sky, the most fantastic light show was taking place, and it was all centred right there as though the clearing was the main stage. As the rider climbed down from his horse, he seemed to turn and smile directly at Ningen. Ningen locked eyes with him, but the rider turned away to address the crowd.

The rider was making a speech of some sort, but it was difficult to make out. In Ningen's ears, the sound was muffled, and he was distracted by the scene around him. He pressed forward, pushing his way through the crowd to get a better look, just in time to hear the rider using *his* name.

"Ningen was stuck because the magic within the tree had bewitched his mind." The rider proclaimed this with confidence, as if teaching a historical fact. "He lost the ability to get back to Kana in the grasslands, but we set him free from his prison, and now he, and his descendants, can know us forevermore."

If it hadn't been a dream, Ningen would have rushed to the rider to embrace him. His words were so kind and so full of hope for his future. But something else going on in the distance stole his attention away. It was the tree, but it was different to how it had looked in real life. It was dark, three times the size, and its branches seemed to be alive, like the wings of a dark bird reaching towards the clearing.

Ningen found himself walking towards the tree. As he went past the rider, the faces of the winged creatures suddenly turned serious, then they started to whip themselves up into a frenzy, as if ready to fight a battle. Panic surrounded Ningen as distressed, warning cries rang out, almost as though they were directed to him. He ignored the cries – he couldn't help himself. He felt unsure about what was happening but found himself calling back to the rider and the crowd that he would be fine. "I'm just going to take a look. I'll be back in a minute."

He made his way out of the clearing and into the grasslands, but the rider and the creatures didn't seem to be able to follow. They screamed and protested and banged at the air as if hitting some kind of wall. As Ningen looked back, the so-called wall became visible. A dark horde of disfigured creatures were rushing to the clearing with force. Above them, a dark warrior flew, shooting through the sky like an arrow. He had wings like shadows at his back and two swords already burnt and red from battle.

Ningen was terrified at the sight, but he had little control of the dream. He wanted to leave, but the tree before him reached its dark, claw-like branches further and grabbed him. At first, he struggled against the force as it dragged him through the fields towards the desert. But as the sweet smell of the roots bewitched his mind again, the screams of the creatures became dull in his ears, replaced instead by the warmth and comfort of the rustling leaves of the tree before him. And as the tree embraced him, Ningen lost all sense of time and fell deeper into spellbound sleep.

When he finally awoke, the sun had already set. He'd somehow managed to sleep for the entire day. Beside him, he could hear the gentle crackling of a wood fire, and the sweet scent of the tree's roots filled his senses.

He smiled to himself and stretched as the warmth and sweet smell filled his heart with contentment.

"Thank goodness that terrible dream is over.

"Wait... I didn't go to sleep by a fire..."

He sat up suddenly and stared around him and, to his absolute horror, realised he was no longer in the woods. Yesterday morning he'd gone for a nap in the woods by the clearing, but somehow, he was now back below the tree in the desert, as though the last day hadn't taken place.

He became aware of a shadow falling somewhere above him, and looked up to the raised ground of the grasslands. He was horrified to see the silhouette of Kana by the tree, the wind blowing her hair in a way that made her look wild and scary.

Kana stood at the edge of the grass, crying her heart out as she looked down at Ningen, trapped in a space she couldn't reach. She knew that setting a single foot on the desert floor was impossible for her. For now, Ningen would have to remain trapped and alone.

Ningen stared back in shocked silence. Before he could call up or offer an explanation, she disappeared from view.

He scrambled to his feet, stamped out the fire, and started to clamber up the bank.

"Kana, wait! I'm sorry!" he shouted with all his might. "It won't happen again, I promise!"

But it was too late. By the time he got to the top of the bank, she was long gone, and he was astonished to see the desert stretching into the distance for as far as the eye could see.

For weeks he'd played in the grasslands, but now they were gone, and Kana with them.

He was well and truly trapped, and all alone in the Desert Dimension, a place of lies and disappointment.

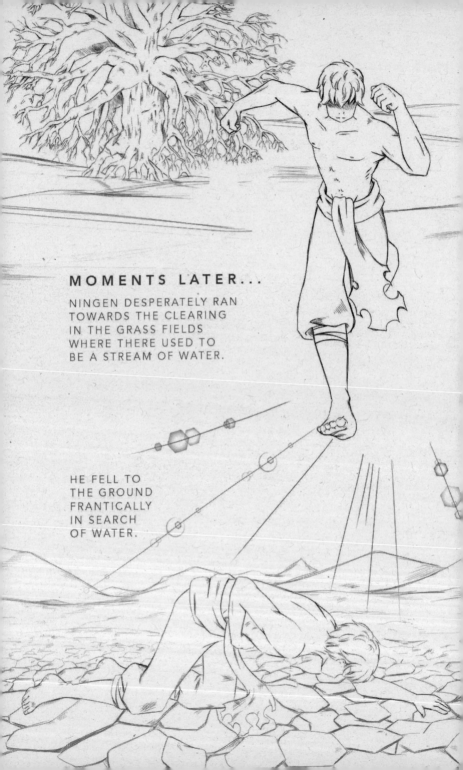

**MOMENTS LATER...**

NINGEN DESPERATELY RAN
TOWARDS THE CLEARING
IN THE GRASS FIELDS
WHERE THERE USED TO
BE A STREAM OF WATER.

HE FELL TO
THE GROUND
FRANTICALLY
IN SEARCH
OF WATER.

**MONTHS
LATER...**

NINGEN WAS
BEGINNING TO
LOSE HIMSELF
IN THE HEAT.

THE ONLY PLACE
OF ESCAPE WAS
UNDER THE TREE.

## CHAPTER FIVE

# TRAPPED

The sun was high in the sky, and there wasn't a cloud to be seen. The desert had been superheated for seven years, and there was no hint of a breeze in the thick, stagnant air.

The landscape was breathtaking, but all you could see were the scars where rivers and waterfalls had once flowed, and the dead wood that lay on the ground where trees had once blossomed. The largest tree was still standing tall, and its great branches were sprawling out, scorched by the sun. It should be impossible for anyone to survive here, but somehow, Ningen was.

The years of heat and loneliness had changed Ningen. He had become a bit odd and had started to act almost cruelly. Whenever he discovered any sign of life, he had no choice but to kill it for food.

Of course, that wasn't how it started. When he first became trapped here, he lived off the roots of the tree, but they were long gone, and the threat of starvation can change a person. Sometimes the heat played tricks on his mind, showing him visions of things that weren't really there. He didn't mind the distraction, though – the odd mirage of a river or an animal was welcome, even if it only lasted for a moment.

On this particular day, Ningen walked across the sandy desert to find water, like he always did. As he roamed, he caught sight of a winged soldier lying unconscious in the sand. At first, he felt sure it was another hallucination, but as he walked towards him, he realised the man was actually there.

The soldier looked dangerous and strong, and Ningen wasn't going to wait for him to wake up. He wasted no time. He grabbed his arm and began to drag him through the desert towards a nearby pit he'd dug earlier in the day. When he reached it, he dropped the limb and shoved the creature in, talking to him as if nothing was wrong the entire time.

"My name's Ningen, by the way."

"As in Nin-gen.

"It's a weird name, I know.

"It sort of matches the situation I'm in at the moment.

"Not my name – I mean how messed up things are.

"Not that it was ever not. Strange, I mean. But yeah, I'm in a real mess…"

The warrior drifted in and out of consciousness as this boy Ningen babbled on about a dream he'd had. The heat was unbearable, and he could feel sand in his teeth. He made a pathetic attempt to clear his throat with the smallest breath, but it made no difference. The boy just interrupted him and continued to talk.

"Save your strength. Who knows, maybe if you concentrate, you might be able to will yourself to a happier place. It's not worked for me yet, but…" Ningen shrugged, "…you never know."

And with that, Ningen patted the warrior on the cheek, got up, brushed the sand off himself, and made his way back to his cave home, obsessing the entire way about how he'd ended up in this position in the first place.

When Ningen arrived back, he was shocked to discover two more men, both lying unconscious like the warrior. These strangers were sunburnt and half conscious. One was facedown, and the other lay sprawled out flat on his back. Terrified, Ningen climbed up to the safety of his tree and anxiously waited for them to wake up.

The constant dry heat had wizened him. His hair was brittle and matted with sand, dirt and sweat, and there was a nervous energy about him. After a short time, he decided he couldn't cope with sitting around and waiting for them, so he broke off a small branch and threw it down at the men. Unfortunately, he threw it in such an awkward way that he lost his footing and fell with a thud to the ground. The men awoke with a jolt, not because of the branch that Ningen threw at them, but because they were startled by his screams of pain.

The first to come round was a scruffy-haired man, holding his head which was throbbing from the heat of the sun. In an instant he regained consciousness and leapt to his feet, breathing heavily in a panic. He spun to the left and right to see where he was. Ningen was so startled by the man's sudden movements that he scurried back to the side of the dead tree, accidentally kicking sand in the other man's face.

Up until this point, the first man hadn't even noticed Ningen. He was more concerned with what was going on, and where he was. He stumbled around for a moment, his head still spinning as his eyes settled and re-focused on his surroundings.

The other man was smartly dressed, almost regal. He was dazed, laid out on his back; but as the sand hit his face, he was forced to focus with such a start that he half choked. As he calmed down and brushed himself off, he noticed the rolling sand disappearing into the distance and became more aware of the furnace-level heat. He glanced briefly across to his companion, but then his attention was drawn to the boy who had thrown sand in his face, who seemed to be trying his hardest to hide away. He tilted his head slightly as it dawned on him who this was. And, with a look on his face that mirrored the confused tone in his voice, he spoke. "Ningen, is that you?"

Ningen scurried back up onto his branch. "How do you know my name?" he shouted.

But before the smart man could answer, he was interrupted. "Hikaru, how did we get here?"

"I'm not sure, Miyako," he slurred, still fixated on Ningen.

"Hey! I asked you a question," said Ningen. "How do you know my name?"

Hikaru smiled as he stood up and shuffled closer to the tree, looking up at Ningen. "It's a long story. But don't worry, I'm not here to hurt you."

Miyako's mind was wandering; he didn't really understand where he was. "Hang on." He tried to refocus. "That man isn't Ningen, is he?"

Miyako and Hikaru looked at each other and then at Ningen, who was now quite agitated.

"Did you do this?" quizzed Miy, as Hikaru reached an arm up towards Ningen.

Hikaru was puzzled by the question, and a bit frustrated. "Did I do this? Are you kidding me? We arrived here together! Anyway, this looks more like something *you* would cause!" Hikaru wasn't usually sarcastic, but it was too hot to play games today.

Miyako sighed. "Look, Ningen is messed up, and to be honest he looks pretty ill."

Miyako's assessment was quite cruel, but at least he was paying attention, thought Hikaru.

Ningen snapped back, "Messed up?" He had no idea what he looked like, but this man he'd never met was being quite rude about him. "Who are you people?"

"I'm so sorry, you must be terrified. My name is Hikaru, and this is Miyako."

Ningen could see that Hikaru was clearly trying to show he was friendly, but Miyako just gave a disinterested salute with a sarcastic grin on his face that somehow matched the way he was dressed.

"Where did you come from?" said Ningen.

Hikaru paused, but Miyako jumped right in. "We came here from the grasslands."

Ningen's heart began to race. "You mean you came from Happiness?"

"From where?" replied Hikaru.

Ningen repeated, "From Happiness. The place on the other side of the desert."

Miyako had started to feel bored, but Ningen's words peaked his interest and he turned to Hikaru. "Is he talking about the different dimensions?"

"Yes, maybe," said Hikaru. "But he's describing them in the same way Kana does."

"He's talking like a child!" mocked Miyako.

Hikaru turned back to the tree and gestured for Miyako to let him speak. "Ningen, if the grasslands are Happiness, what would you describe this desert as?"

Ningen took a moment, and his face fell. "This is Disappointment. It's where you get trapped when you lie, and when you cheat. That's what Kana told me, anyway. Is that why you're here? Did you do something wrong too?"

Miyako sniggered a little under his breath, but Hikaru simply said, "No. I'm here to take you to a new, better place. I'm here to take you home."

"And what about him?" Ningen nodded towards Miyako, which didn't seem to go down very well with him. It was clear to Ningen that although Hikaru and Miyako were there together, they were nothing alike. Hikaru acted with kindness, and was dressed in a royal robe, but Miyako was dressed like an adventurer and acted like talking to him was a chore. That is, he acted like it was a chore until the moment Ningen suggested he may be a liar.

Miyako snarled, ran at the tree with force, then began scaling it effortlessly. Ningen tried his best to get away, but Miyako was too fast for him. As he scrambled onto Ningen's branch, he bounced on it slightly as if to scare him.

"Be careful!" shouted Hikaru, afraid for their safety.

Ningen wobbled forward and let out a scream as Miyako caught him in his arms.

Miyako laughed and patted Ningen on the back like a pet. "Look, Hikaru, he's fine!" His eyes narrowed in a mean smile.

"Just… please come down," replied Hikaru, his patience wearing thin. "And… Miyako?"

"Yeah?" Miy responded.

"Try to bring him with you."

Miyako was as cunning as he was agile and, waiting for Hikaru to move around the side of the tree to help, he set to work on the real reason he had caught up with Ningen. He pulled the boy closer and whispered in his ear, "That man will help you. But mind him – doesn't he seem like he'd keep things from you?" And at that, Miyako leapt down from the tree, leaving Ningen dazed and confused on the branch. "Sorry, Hikaru, he doesn't want to come down," he said as he landed, the sly grin still stamped on his face.

Hikaru didn't believe him, but he was happy to play along for now. He drew close to Miy and stood in front of him so that Ningen couldn't hear what he was about to whisper. "Miy, listen… he doesn't know who we are. He's scared, so just—"

"Scared? Yeah, I bet he's terrified!" Miy laughed scornfully. He couldn't care less whether Ningen was scared or not. "I told you he was a bad idea," he blustered as he pointed up to the branch.

Hikaru didn't agree, "Miy, Ningen was a wonderful idea…"

As they spoke, Ningen dropped silently down from the tree behind them. Even though they were whispering, he had overheard some of what they said. What Miyako had said to him up on the branch had already worried him, and now it looked as if this man, Hikaru, might be plotting something with Miyako. Still, it felt like Hikaru had nothing but love for both Ningen and Miyako, and it showed on his face.

Miy wasn't feeling at all sentimental but could see that Hikaru was lost in the moment as he spotted Ningen on the ground and started towards him. Miy looked around him some more, musing. "There's something about this desert that feels so familiar." In the distance, all he could see were desert plains, but for a moment he thought he could see a flag waving, as if a gust of wind had moved it. "There's a flag!" he shouted. "A flag in the distance." He turned, trying to get Hikaru's attention, but then a familiar feeling rose within him, leaving him completely speechless. He felt himself suddenly weightless...

Ningen was already struggling to cope with the events of the day, but this was something else. As he watched, Miyako disappeared into thin air. "Where did he go?"

Hikaru sighed and tried his best to explain. "You need to understand, Ningen, Miyako and I have magic within us. We're not the same, but we're both able to do some quite incredible things."

"Like what?" Ningen was intrigued. Kana was magic too, but he hadn't ever felt like there was anything special inside him.

"Let's try and just get to know each other a bit better, shall we? You can find out more in time. And don't worry about Miyako – sometimes he just disappears." Hikaru knew far more than he was letting on but tried his hardest to move the conversation on. "It's best to just let him do what he wants to do. Forget about him – he'll come back when he's ready. Anyway, why don't you show me where you live?"

## CHAPTER SIX

# DISCOVERY

Miyako regained his composure quickly. Hikaru was right about him being magic, but vanishing into thin air was not something he enjoyed. It was disorientating, and he didn't feel in control of it. Still, if it worked to his advantage, he wasn't going to complain.

He glanced at the ground and reeled, shocked to see the gagged head of a Tenshi warrior sticking out of the sand at his feet.

The Tenshi were Royal Guards. Servants of Kana, Hikaru, and their sister Seirei.

All three of them could be frustrating at times, but although he was jealous of her wings, Miy actually got on quite well with Seirei. Not that she would have it any other way – she was too strong for him to argue with and very sure of what she wanted.

Hikaru was a different story, but Miy didn't much care for him. Seirei was a beautiful, powerful woman with majestic wings, but Hikaru was just a man of average height. A dynamic man, whose words carried mystical powers – but who cares? It's not as if he could fly or anything.

And then there was Kana.

Nothing could compare to her. She was magnificent, and she resounded with the pure power of creation.

"Tenshi, wake up!" he exclaimed in a panic, ripping the gag from the man's mouth. "What happened here?"

"It was Ningen, sir," he panted. "He's gone wild. Quick, dig me out so I can fly us away."

Miy stared at him in disbelief as he thought back to what he'd said to Ningen in the tree. "That man will help you. But mind him – doesn't he seem like he'd keep things from you?"

Miyako's power was rooted in persuasion. At its best, he could command the entire Royal Guard in service of Kana, Hikaru and Seirei. But Miyako was tricky, and if he wanted to, he could convince you lies were true – even lies about yourself.

"What do you mean, Ningen's gone wild?" he responded. "He's a bit odd, yes – but I was just with him! He seemed okay to me."

"No, sir," replied the warrior. "Ningen dragged me through the desert and trapped me in this hole. He acted the entire time like he was just talking to a friend. He's lost his mind!"

Miyako began digging furiously as the Tenshi warrior wriggled to get free. The Tenshi was in a vulnerable position in the sand and leaving him would have been easy, but honestly, what would be the point? He was as stuck as the Tenshi was. Except the warrior had wings that could fly them away.

Before all of this, Miyako had been a Tenshi, serving as the leader of the Royal Guard for Kana, Hikaru, and Seirei. When they were together, the Tenshi called them

*The One* because they did everything as one and their power was linked. As Miyako dug, his mind took him back to those days when everything felt perfect in the Eternal Dimension, and light surrounded everything.

"Sir?" the Tenshi blustered, snapping Miyako out of his daydream. "Are you here alone, sir? Is Hikaru here too?"

Miy looked deep into his eyes, and a serious look came over his face as he thought through what he was going to say. He knew that back at the tree Hikaru would be helping Ningen, trying to make something out of the situation.

Despite the ease of their interaction, there was something far darker going on here than Ningen or this Tenshi could know. There was no doubt that Hikaru was here to take Ningen to a better place, but that wasn't true for Miyako. He couldn't have cared less about Ningen, or Hikaru for that matter.

Eventually, after what seemed like an age, Miyako spoke. "No. If Hikaru is here, I've not seen him. I'm alone."

CHAPTER SEVEN

# CAVE PAINTINGS

Inside Ningen's cave, there was a considerable amount of space. It was about eight feet deep and could comfortably sit a few people. It looked as if the whole root structure of the tree above had been cleared out, leaving open space where the soil had once been.

Hikaru made his way in and scanned the area. Scorch marks from Ningen's fires scarred the ground, and piles of discarded tree bark and dried roots were strewn all over the floor. Above them, the ceiling was peppered with holes, some large enough to see right through to the trunk of the tree above.

On the walls, large scenes were painted in dirt, depicting a life long since gone. The first showed trees, stars in the sky, and two people drawn in a way that made them look like they were dancing. The mural was beautiful and full of peace. The second one, merging almost seamlessly with the first, showed a meal, and again, the two were together laughing and happily sharing stories as they ate.

The third painting was more significant than the others: huge, sprawling shapes danced in a dazzling skyscape of clouds, expressing the very best of times and capturing a deep feeling of contentment. As that painting finished, though, the fourth revealed a darker tale. First, there was an image of winged men, with one standing taller and grander than the others. As Hikaru's gaze moved along the painting, he made out a huge dirt scribble that seemed to indicate a battle of sorts. Next, a giant tree monster appeared to be reaching out and holding a man in the air, clearly against his will, and the man reached back towards the winged group.

The next image was even more chaotic. One figure sat beneath a tree, eating alone, while another floated in the sky above. The figure in the sky had clearly been thrown up onto the wall while Ningen was in some pain. The strokes were harsh, and her hair coiled out from her head like vipers, her eyes black as night. She was hurling bolts of lightning and fire that scorched the ground.

Next came a painting that might have been the oldest of them all. It had been scratched at and mostly destroyed, but Hikaru could clearly see that this had initially been a beautiful painting of Kana.

The last time Hikaru had been with Kana was just before Ningen first opened his eyes. "I know life has been difficult for you, Ningen, but things here are far worse than I ever imagined."

## CHAPTER EIGHT

# THE MIRACLE

"I'm so pleased to have you here, Hikaru. I've never had anyone in my home before."

Ningen was happy to have the company. Still, after what Miyako had said to him, he was also feeling anxious, and as he tried desperately to keep Hikaru in sight while he organised himself, he stumbled over and found himself in a heap on the floor, bleeding from his head and clutching his leg.

Hikaru rushed over, full of compassion for him. He lifted him to his feet, closed his eyes and began to say words that sounded like magic. "Kana, I know you can hear me. Ningen needs you. Move through me now and restore him." Hikaru breathed slowly over Ningen. "Ningen, you were made to be whole, and you were made for a wonderful purpose."

Hikaru's words, as simple as they were, hit the air around them like a sledgehammer. He had been flagging from the heat, and wearier than usual since being cut off from Kana; however, the moment Hikaru spoke, it was like a torch burst into flame. They were suddenly bathed in light, which transformed the dark, under-tree cave into a luminescent new creation.

First, the ground under their feet bloomed with lush green grass, and there was a dampness to it that was so welcome in the heat. Next, vines with multicoloured flowers began to weave around the cave and spring from every dark corner. Despite Ningen's lingering worries about Hikaru, he couldn't help but be in awe at the spectacular transformation of everything around him.

Finally, Ningen began to sense a strange warmth in his head and leg. Although Hikaru had been holding him the entire time, the warmth didn't seem to be coming from his hands. It was his words that were changing the atmosphere, and now they were pouring out of him. As the words washed over Ningen, he felt all the pain throughout his entire body fade away to nothing. He hadn't even realised he'd been hurting so badly, but now he could see there was far more wrong with him than just these superficial pains.

When Hikaru finished speaking, not only was Ningen healed, but everything around them was beautifully restored, and Ningen was absolutely mesmerised, beaming from ear to ear.

He took a moment to compose himself. How could this have happened? How had this one man achieved all of this just by speaking? He stretched himself out, flexed his muscles and bent his back in ways that he wasn't able to before. He thought about how incredible this all was. He ran his hands over the beautiful foliage surrounding them and smiled.

Yet, despite this fantastic experience, it was hard to forget what he had been through recently. He thought back to the warrior he'd trapped in the desert, and the feeling of pure calm began to slowly fade away as it made space for even more guilt.

But maybe, just maybe, Hikaru could be trusted.

Maybe this was a good time to find out if Hikaru could help.

# CHAPTER NINE

# WILDERNESS

Hikaru sat back and smiled at their vibrant new surroundings. "What would you like to do, Ningen? Is there anything else you'd like me to do for you?"

"Right. Well, I do need to check on something," replied Ningen, thinking about the warrior. "Would you like to come?"

Hikaru was keen to know Ningen better, so they climbed out of the tree-cave and began to make their way to the other side of the desert.

As they walked, Ningen told Hikaru about the whole adventure, glamourising it as he unfolded the tale. "You know, at first I thought he was dead, but he moved a bit, so I tied him up and lowered him into a pit."

Ningen didn't describe his prisoner in much detail. Still, Hikaru was worried that he might have trapped a Royal Guard.

Ningen continued. "I actually hurt myself quite badly. I limped all the way back to my tree – I was in so much pain – and then when I got back…" he paused, "… there you guys were."

As Ningen uttered the words, all his newfound energy and confidence in Hikaru seemed to melt away, and he began to worry that everything might be connected. For all his bluster, Ningen was quite simple, and it was only now he was starting to piece it all together. A winged creature and two men. What if there were more? What if they were friends? And where did the other man go?

While Ningen spoke, Hikaru began to worry that Ningen may have done something terrible, but, being as wise as he was strong, he decided to try to figure out who Ningen had become as they walked through the desert. He struck up a new conversation, hoping to find out whether Ningen remembered Kana. "Do you remember how you got here?"

"No," replied Ningen. "I've just always been here, I think. I do remember there used to be more plants and things, but something must have happened."

Hikaru knew Ningen must have found out how to lure the magic from the tree. The magic was wonderful but would have ruined his relationship with Kana. "Do you know... at your lowest point, you still had everything you were created for right inside you, Ningen?"

Ningen shifted uncomfortably, getting increasingly nervous again. If Miyako was right, then Hikaru was holding something back from him. As they walked, he thought for a moment before responding.

"Do you know," he said eventually, "with your power, you could transform all of this?" He gestured to the arid landscape.

Hikaru's stomach turned as Ningen spoke. Was he trying to tempt him to perform? That was something he would have expected from Miyako. "I could," he said, masking his shock with a smile, "but that's not what my power's for."

"You could make us some food."

Hikaru could see that Ningen was trying to get him to do amazing things, but instead he laughed it off and changed the subject. "There's nothing more precious than you, Ningen; nothing in all of creation."

"Really?" Ningen snapped back, stopping suddenly and turning to stare at Hikaru. "You could probably throw yourself off the rocks over there and not die, and you say I'm the most precious?"

Hikaru stopped too, shocked by his jibe. "I'd gladly die, Ningen. I'll have to one day soon." A look of sadness crumpled his face as he whispered to himself, "It's how I'm going to get you out of here."

Ningen was confused. This conversation had taken an unexpected turn, and he didn't want to ask any more questions about what Hikaru meant. He trudged onwards, and soon they spotted the watering hole in the distance, close to where Ningen had trapped his prisoner.

## CHAPTER TEN

# STUCK

At first Ningen didn't notice the new mound of sand close to the pit, but as they drew a little closer, it became clear to him that the warrior had gone. "Oh no!" He rushed forward in a panic, leaving Hikaru strolling alone, wondering what he was supposed to be seeing.

Ningen ran so far and so fast he didn't notice the looming shadow hurtling towards them from the sky. Hikaru was still far away, but he was the first to become aware of the Tenshi warrior carrying Miyako beneath him.

"Look, they're down there! Drop me now!" screamed Miyako as he whooshed over Hikaru's head.

"Yes, sir!" shouted the Tenshi, and at that, he let him go.

In an instant, Miy was falling from the sky in such a way it looked like he was flying. He stretched out his arms, relishing the moment. Ningen, now in a full sprint and aware of the winged man above, hadn't noticed him. As Ningen skidded to a stop by the pit, Miyako landed with a roll and appeared right in front of him.

Ningen gasped in amazement as Miy launched himself at him with an angry snarl. In the next moment, the sky flashed with lightning, the bolts lighting up the darkness to reveal a tall, winged warrior woman thundering to the ground. She landed, erupting the ground into a sand explosion behind Hikaru. Miyako knew precisely who this was, and who was coming next.

He wasted no time. He grabbed Ningen around the back of his neck and pulled his ear close to his mouth.

Hikaru was gazing at the warrior woman. "Seirei, thank goodness you're here!"

Seirei clapped her wings together in front of her, and as Hikaru felt the magical, life-giving torrent of air resounding around him, he closed his eyes and summoned yet another person.

But he was too late.

Miyako had already begun to whisper his magic to Ningen. "Don't you feel ashamed of what you've done?"

Ningen was dazed, and snapped right back, shaking off Miy's words. "What do you mean?"

"I mean, you're a mess, and the fact you live in the desert just confirms how much of a failure you are."

As they argued, a third person began to materialise before them, and Hikaru rushed over towards Ningen. "Miy!" he shouted. "You've got to leave Ningen alone. We're trying to help him."

Miyako shoved Ningen closer to the edge of the pit. "I'm not interested in helping. I hate everything about him."

Ningen could barely hold Miyako back, and scrambled through the sand to keep from falling. Out of the corner of his eye he caught a glimpse of the new person who'd just appeared from nowhere. It couldn't be. It was! His old friend Kana! "Kana, is that you?"

"It is!" called Hikaru. "Keep fighting, Ningen! Don't give up."

"And what about me?" screamed Miyako.

"We can make all of this right, Miy," said Seirei, "but you need to leave Ningen alone!"

"What's happening?" exclaimed Hikaru, turning back to where Kana was standing. She was only half visible, as if behind some kind of glass wall.

Seirei dashed over to help. "Why can't she appear? Kana, what's wrong?"

"Seirei, go and help Ningen," urged Hikaru.

But before she could reach him, Miyako kicked out for a final time and sent Ningen plummeting headlong into the pit.

The sound Kana was making was hardly audible,
but cracks and snaps rang out from the midst of
something that was beginning to look like a cloud holding
her presence.

Hikaru looked at Miyako, and his face became stern.
"What have you done?" he demanded, with more than
a hint of accusation in his tone.

Miy was incensed. "I've done what needed to be done!"

The cloud pulsed and began to grow larger as they
argued. "What do you mean by that?" snapped Hikaru.

Rage boiled inside Miyako, and he flung his answer at Hikaru with force. "You were supposed to love me!" Miyako paused and refocused, but he was distracted by the storm that was starting to rage around the cloud, as well as the frantic shouts from Seirei.

"Ningen, take my hand! Come on… wake up!"

But Ningen lay helplessly inside the pit, as if trapped in some sort of trance. "Hikaru, he won't reach for me!" Seirei sobbed. "Ningen, come on!"

Rain and thunder raged all around them, and Ningen was fast becoming submerged in the surging water and sand. Seirei cried out in desperation.

"Seirei, come away!" shouted Hikaru. "This isn't the end for Ningen!"

In the next moment, the cloud flashed and the ground around them began to harden as the air rapidly cooled. The cloud sparked, and suddenly Ningen was frozen, locked away within his pit as the crackling cloud disappeared, taking Kana back to the Eternal Dimension.

"Hikaru!" huffed Miyako, as if challenging his authority. "The next time we meet, I'm gonna sort Ningen out for good." As he spoke, his breath froze in the air around him, creating an eerie mist. "I'm going to kill him, and then I'm going to make you wish you'd never started any of this."

And with that, Miyako was gone.

## CHAPTER ELEVEN
# MINUTES EARLIER

Ningen stood, braced, fighting to stay out of the pit. Miyako's flailing arms and accusations were more than he could bear.

The scene was charged, wild, and utterly chaotic. Still, nothing could prepare Ningen for the tall, beautiful warrior who appeared as if from nowhere. As she landed, she burst apart the ground and flexed her mighty wings.

Ningen was using all his strength against Miyako and only caught a glimpse of her. Hikaru rushed over and cried out the name Ningen had been longing to hear every moment since the day he'd got trapped in the desert wilderness. "Kana."

The name gushed through the air like a tidal wave, and Miyako began to buckle under the pressure.

Ningen shouted with everything he had within him, pushing and grappling against the now seemingly weakened Miyako. That's when he caught a glimpse of her, and a rush of warmth spread through him. "Kana, is that you?"

"It is," replied Hikaru, willing Ningen to hold on. "Keep fighting, Ningen! Don't give up!"

Both Ningen and Miyako were exhausted from the heat and the struggle. Hearing Hikaru's support was just what Ningen needed, but to Miyako it was the last straw. He smirked, looked Ningen right in the face, and then withdrew slightly, causing him to stumble forward. Then Miyako made his move. He leapt back at him and kicked him with such force it sent him plummeting headlong into the pit.

## CHAPTER TWELVE

# THE FALL

"Time, as it happens, doesn't move the same when you're falling.

"As I fell, I could see everything with sharp clarity. There was Miyako, practically growling, breathing heavily over the pit, while that winged warrior woman lunged forward to grab at me as I fell. I think they called her Siri, or was it Say-ray?" Thought Ningen.

Hikaru was gazing at them as if to ensure she was successfully rescuing him, but Kana looked on from a pulsating, crackling, terrifying cloud, somehow smiling as if everything was perfectly normal. "I can't believe it," Ningen muttered. "I waited to see her for so long, and now I'm probably going to die."

Ningen could see an almost full range of emotions flickering over the faces of the four above him, but there was a difficult truth he couldn't shake. He was falling for far too long, and there didn't seem to be an end to it.

As moments turned to seconds, and seconds turned to minutes, Ningen became aware that heat had turned to cold and, as the freeze set in, light was gently morphing to dusk, until he realised all at once that he wasn't falling at all.

Ningen was laid flat on a hard, cold stone slab.

He mused to himself for a moment. "Have I been talking to myself again?"

Just then, a shiver rippled through his whole body, and he jumped to his feet. Unfortunately, before he could focus his eyes enough to try and see anything in the dark, he felt a foggy faintness wrapping itself around his head, and he collapsed right back onto the slab where he had landed.

"Yes!" A voice rang out in the dark. "You have been talking to yourself. And you do every night."

The voice sounded tired, and quite broken, but it continued, despite the silence on the other end of the conversation. "Get some rest, Ningen. It's not over yet."

## CHAPTER THIRTEEN

# STONE

The Stone Dimension was a prison guarded by the fallen Tenshi warriors who were known as the Horde. There was no light here, although you could see. It was like dusk – the kind of half-light that plays tricks on your mind and gives you nightmares.

In the dark, a dusky beam emitted its terrifying light across the stone landscape. In the shadows, groups of Horde creatures were huddled and lying in wait for any kind of food to unwittingly stumble into their grasp.

The Horde were like packs of hyenas. At one time, they had been majestic Royal Tenshi warriors, servants of Kana, Hikaru and Seirei. But now they were twisted, broken, and hungry for flesh. Where mighty wings had once sprouted proudly from their backs, broken stumps were now all that remained. Their armour was all but completely gone, and in its place, matted hair partially covered what had become calloused skin.

In their prime, these soldiers had walked tall, but now they were stooped, some crawling on all fours, clawing their way around, pulling and ripping at each other as if nothing mattered anymore.

The Horde had to learn to see in the thick blackness, and over time their eyes adjusted for spying through the dark. Unfortunately, this was not the case for Ningen or the stranger in the darkness.

"I don't know if you can hear me?" said Ningen softly. "I fell, but I don't know where I am."

He had no reference for what he was experiencing. It was so dark, and he was colder than he'd ever been before. As he spoke, the strangest thing was happening. It was as if all his words were being bounced back at him from unseen spaces. Of course, it was simply an echo, but he had never heard such a thing in the grasslands or in the desert.

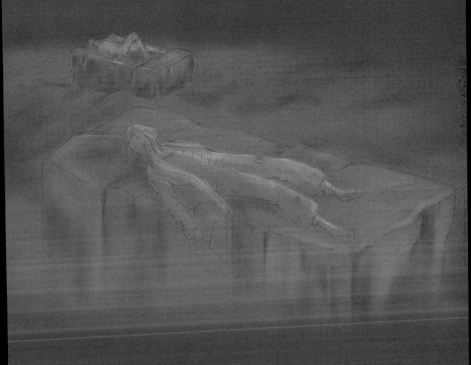

"I thought I heard someone there?" he called out, only to recoil as he heard the tail end of his sentence rebounding at him in ever-decreasing echoes. "Someone there? Someone there? Someone there?"

"I'm not going to give up!" he declared to himself. This time, the echo seemed to cruelly mock him. "Give up… give up… give up… give up…"

"Don't give up, my friend." Another voice cut through the darkness, then lowered to a whisper. "But do be quiet. There're things in here that would eat you if they found you." The voice paused. "Now, save your strength. Sleep, if you can. We're not going to be here long."

Ningen froze; that voice sounded familiar. It sounded like Hikaru… but how could that be? In any case, with that warping echoing in his ears, he didn't dare say another word. He lay down, trying to get comfortable, and closed his eyes, hoping sleep would come.

Hikaru knew well enough who the Horde were and what they guarded. But they didn't seem to be around at the moment, though he couldn't quite figure out where else they could be; there were no structures or dimensions or other places they could go to. Fallen Tenshi had no wings and so couldn't travel anywhere. In some ways, they were as much stuck in this stone prison as Hikaru and Ningen were – if they were here, that was. But he knew that if they were, he and Ningen would be vulnerable.

After some time mulling on these things, he stood up to try to make his way over to Ningen. "I'm coming over," he whispered in the smallest voice he had. But as quiet as he was, his words bounced around the shadowed stone and came back to him as fresh as he'd said them. "Ningen!" he whispered cautiously. "Ningen, are you awake? You need to be ready to go."

Ningen didn't answer but stirred where he lay. He'd fallen asleep.

Thkard took a couple of tentative steps away from the slab he'd been standing on and, with an almighty crash, was shoved back onto the ground by an invisible force. He didn't see anything, but it was like there was a wall stopping him from going further. He got up, brushed himself down, and tried a different angle. But again, he was forcibly knocked down. This time, however, he was sure he felt a fist, and as he was pushed back, he saw a shadow flicker past him.

"Who is it? Who's there?" Hikaru said, somewhat fearful that he might be hit again. He scrambled back to his feet and stepped forward, reaching out cautiously to feel his way. He stopped, puzzled, as he bumped into something once again. To his amazement, he felt something like a body in front of him, barricading him. He couldn't see it, but it was definitely there. He carefully circled the stone slab, gently pushing at intervals to see what was happening.

More of them. All around him, at every angle.

He was completely surrounded.

Hikaru's heart pounded in his chest. This was not what he was used to. Defeat certainly wasn't an option; he'd come too far with Ningen. But for now, he had no choice but to sit back down, thankful at least that whatever was messing with him was leaving Ningen alone.

## CHAPTER FOURTEEN

# THE KEY

As Hikaru lay puzzling over their situation, Ningen woke himself up screaming from a nightmare. His scream erupted with such force that the sound almost shook the sky. Hikaru sat bolt upright in terror. "Ningen, it's me, Hikaru. You're okay… just please don't move!"

Ningen was disorientated and panting heavily. "What do you mean, don't move? Hikaru, I fell down a pit! How did I get here?"

"It's difficult to explain," replied Hikaru. "You've actually been here for years."

"Years!" exclaimed Ningen. "How have I been here for years?"

"Listen." Hikaru lowered his voice. "You once told me that Kana described places as feelings, yes? You described the grasslands as a place where you were happy, and the desert wilderness as disappointing. Well... this place is a dead end. Time means nothing here."

"If that's true, then how come you're here?"

"I came here for you. I'm here to take you to a better place."

Ningen made a scornful face and reflected it in his tone. "You said that before. You told me that in the wilderness. Why should I believe you now?"

"Because the better place..." Hikaru paused for a moment, "...is on the other side of the dead end."

Ningen was confused. "The other side?"

"Yes. On the other side of the Stone Dimension is a place of pure, wonderful life. Kana actually calls it Love, but she exaggerates all the time. It's really just the place you were born."

Ningen thought for a moment. "The grasslands are on the other side of this place?"

"That's right." As Hikaru spoke, he thought he heard something scratching in the unseen darkness. Maybe the barrier he'd felt before?

"Hikaru?" whispered Ningen. "If I've been here for years, how did you get—"

"I died," Hikaru interrupted forcibly. "I know it's hard to understand but I was there with Kana before you were born. We were together but Miyako tried to hurt you. Then I met you in the desert wilderness and we've been trying to help you ever since. Now, stay where you are. I'm going to try to come to you." He gathered himself, took a deep breath and, in one swift movement, launched himself towards Ningen.

But as he lunged forward, the invisible wall of beings he'd encountered before stopped him effortlessly. One by one, kicks and punches knocked him back and forth, leaving him with no control.

Ningen didn't understand what was happening, but he remained where he was. He couldn't stay quiet, however. "Hikaru! Hikaru!" His calls turned to screams from the very pit of his stomach as the fight got louder. "HIKARU!"

It didn't help his cause, but Hikaru was encouraged by his concern.

Hikaru tried his hardest not to return the creatures' violence, but in a moment of deep pain and rage, he screeched and hit out at them.

"YOU COWARDS! SHOW YOURSELVES!"

And at that, the horde of fallen Tenshi materialised in front of him, growling and prowling around like hungry wolves, salivating as they glared at him.

Hikaru froze, and Ningen collapsed in absolute terror at the sight. They had never been more afraid in their lives.

"Do you remember me, Tenshi?" Hikaru said to the closest fallen warrior, recoiling as its rancid breath coursed over his face.

No response.

Instead, the Horde attacked him again and bundled him back onto the slab, punching and kicking him with all the hatred and contempt they held inside.

Hikaru was overwhelmed, but he wasn't just going to take it. He wouldn't fight, but maybe he would still be able to use whatever magic he had left. He closed his eyes through the pain and concentrated hard before summoning everything he had.

"Tenshi, remember who you are! Remember who you were created to serve!"

His words severed the Horde's control with devastating effectiveness – his magic scattered them and smashed the stone slab beneath him. But instead of setting him free, the broken slab revealed a blinding shaft of eerie light that trapped him in a more intense way than before.

His vision was obscured by the light, and he was somehow frozen, suspended in the air and unable to move a muscle.

The Horde were dazed and confused, but they rapidly raised themselves back up and started forming regimented lines, as if preparing to welcome a superior being.

"You died and no longer exist, Hikaru," the Horde chanted.

Ningen rubbed his throbbing head, his mind racing. "Hikaru died?" His face crumpled in confusion. "But he said he came here for me? Why would he do that?"

"I died to free Ningen!" Hikaru cried back at the Horde.

They persisted. "You've forfeited yourself, and now neither you or Ningen can leave the dimension of stone."

"I can leave," he protested. "I'm Hikaru, the *name above all names*!"

"The *name above all names* does not exist here; he cannot. If he were here, he would be trapped forever."

"But I *am* here, and I need to leave. I'm taking Ningen out of this place!"

"Only the holder of the key may leave," recited the Horde as one. "Only the key will do. Only the key will release you."

The Horde's chants went on and on as they swayed menacingly. "Only the key. Only the key. Only the key. Only the key…"

Hikaru was bound by the evil light. He felt so close to leaving the Stone Dimension, but it was useless. His body was completely trapped, and all he could do was scream for them to stop.

Ningen sat, traumatised, shaking and trying to block out the experience. "Please stop!" he pleaded. "I didn't mean for any of this to happen." He begged the creatures to stop their incessant chanting. "Hikaru, I'm sorry… it's all my fault—"

"It isn't!" cried Hikaru. "You couldn't have known. It's not all your fault."

In the next moment, the chanting suddenly stopped short, and Hikaru's last words rang out: "All your fault… all your fault… all your fault…"

But as the words got lost in the echoey distance, they were replaced with a lone, slow, mocking laugh that came from another familiar voice. By this point Ningen had lost the ability to be shocked. He was now a mere passenger in a journey he'd lost complete control of. Who was this now? And what did he want?

"I'm sorry," mocked the stranger from the shadows. "I don't mean to laugh. I just can't believe we managed to trap you, Hikaru. Surely it should be impossible to do that!"

Hikaru always knew more than he let on, but the speaker wasn't wrong. Hikaru shouldn't be able to be caught like this. "I did wonder if you were listening …" he said, before naming the man, "Miyako."

"I've been watching you ever since Ningen was created." Miyako snarled, his lips curling.

"And you think I don't know that?" said Hikaru. "I know what you've been doing, Miyako. Not that it matters now."

Miyako drifted closer to Hikaru, rising up to make himself taller and more imposing than him. "Knowing something doesn't give you power, Hikaru."

"You're right, but at least whatever power I have comes from me. Your power comes from the worst magic imaginable. Anyway, you only ever existed to serve me, and it won't be long before you're removed from existence all together."

"That's interesting." Miyako paused, then started hissing, "All your fault… all your fault… all your fault," as if bringing back the echo to taunt Hikaru some more. "I thought I existed to kill Ningen?" He came to a pause again for a few moments, then snarled under his breath, "Well, either way, I've stopped *you*, and I didn't even try to do that!"

"I gave my life for Ningen. And Kana will be here to take us away any minute now."

Miyako didn't fully understand Kana's power, but at the mention of her name, the Horde around him began to bow and withdraw.

"There you go," said Hikaru. "The Horde understand! Kana's coming."

But Miy wasn't convinced. "I think we both know Kana isn't coming, Hikaru. She couldn't even save Ningen from the desert. How would she suddenly be able to come here? To the dead end?"

"I don't care what you think," cried Hikaru. "Kana and Seirei are both coming. They're coming here to take me home, and I'm taking Ningen with me."

Whenever Hikaru mentioned Kana and Seirei, the Horde seemed to lose more of their confidence, but Miyako remained resolute. Hikaru continued to push and argue from his prison of light and, as he spoke, the truth burst from inside him like a powerful explosion.

"I am Hikaru, I am Kana, and *I am* Seirei!"

At his words, the Horde cringed further back, and Hikaru grew in confidence. "I am *The One*. The beginning and the end."

You're in trouble now!" shouted a suddenly excited Ningen. He was still too afraid to move from his slab, but he was up on his feet and beginning to feel like the tables were turning in their favour.

And then it came to Hikaru like a flash – as every fibre of his being reached out for control of the light that was entrapping him. His eyes blazed red like fire, and words like a double-edged sword came shooting from his mouth. "*I am* the key!" he shouted.

The light began to change into something else. Something good. It poured down through all the cracks, illuminating the shadows, bathing Hikaru and finally forming into the shape of Seirei's wings at his back. "I am the key to eternal life."

In his hands, the ultimate power of creation flashed like lightning. "I am *The One*. This is how all of creation will know I am the *King of the Eternal Dimension*. The *name above all names*. I was dead. But now I'm alive. I'm the key to all fullness and all life."

In an instant, Hikaru began to shine like the brightest sun, banishing Miyako into nothingness with the force of the light. As the moment pressed on, the Horde scattered, completely disorientated, and before they could compose themselves, Hikaru and Ningen were gone.

## CHAPTER FIFTEEN

# A BETTER PLACE

There was no other way to explain it. Ningen's life had been very odd. Still, this moment was possibly the one he could explain the least.

Only moments after being rescued from the Stone Dimension, he was standing in a rapidly changing landscape. Hikaru was nowhere to be seen, which was a shame. After what they'd been through, this would have been a great time to celebrate!

Around Ningen, a miraculous transformation was still taking place. New life was blooming all around him. Water, which had been lying in scattered puddles underfoot, was separating around other areas of the ground, and grass was springing up in fresh, sweet-smelling clumps, as if by magic.

Ningen wandered through the landscape, and with every step more flowers blossomed, more trees and bushes flourished, more streams and rivers flowed. It was like the stories that Kana had once told him.

"Imagine if every step you take were a step of creation," she would say. "Imagine if colours and smells and joy and love sprang from the very ground you were playing on."

He began to run faster in the clearing, prancing and dancing as he spun round and round, his arms flung wide as he relished the freedom of the moment. He circled around as dust and dirt whipped up like a swirling cloud in the centre of the clearing. Then, as if he'd summoned her from the power of his dance, Ningen was sure Kana was becoming visible in the cloud. In a moment her hand was already in his as he bounced around, laughing and whooping in the joy of it all.

But this beauty wasn't Kana at all.

His dance was fast and exciting, but he had no magic within himself whatsoever. This beautiful woman had sprung up from the ground. She'd appeared as a new creation, an expression of the perfection that was brought on by the death of the *King of the Eternal Dimension*. She was like Ningen, but born again. And so, as the cloud cleared, he stopped and stared at her, his hand still awkwardly clasping hers as he gulped and let out a dry-mouthed "Whoa!"

At the other end of the landscape, a dip led down to a brand new area. In the grasslands, this had been a desert – dangerous and off limits. But now an amazing, clear-blue sea expanded far into the distance, carrying a fresh breeze and the smell of adventure to the shore.

On the edge of the dip, there was hardly a trace of the tree that had once stood there. As this new place took shape, the ground was becoming green and fertile again, but the soil where the tree had stood was brown and lifeless. Grass surrounded the area, but nothing alive now crossed the line where the tree should have been.

However, while Ningen got to know this new person in his life, the soil would eventually begin to break, exposing the tiniest shoot of what would become a brand new, beautiful tree.

CHAPTER SIXTEEN

# LOVE SONG

Weeks had passed since Hikaru saved Ningen from the Stone Dimension. Ningen returned to life, but Hikaru was still nowhere to be found. In the grasslands, Ningen wasn't allowed past the tree, and in the desert the cave was a sign of his failure, but now he sat freely in the mouth of his cave, enjoying the time passing by as the water lapped peacefully by the shore. Above him, verdant roots pushed slowly but surely down into the soil, and the shoot of what would become another majestic tree held on tight in the fresh sea breeze.

Ningen had been through a lot, and now he was trying to make sense of having a new companion in his life. She was quite something to behold; confident, capable, and full of plans for how they would spend their future.

If he were honest, her plans did make him feel happy. But he was worried. His memory of life with Kana was very sketchy, but the artwork in his cave told the story of how he wasn't someone who was good at being trusted. Still, this new relationship was different to the one he'd had with Kana. Kana was more like a mum and a playmate, but this woman, well, she made him feel giddy.

On the first day they met, he learnt that she loved to sing, and so he called her Aika, which means *love song*. He sat for practically the first full day she was there, staring at her and listening to her make up songs. Even now, down by the shore, her song resounded on the air. It calmed him and, as he lay down, listening to the lapping water and the sweet melody of her song, he drifted off to sleep.

In the clearing, Aika was enjoying the warm breeze that gently rustled the trees around her. The sound of the swaying leaves was rhythmic and sounded like a song.

Aika was different to Ningen. When he was created from the ground, he didn't know or understand anything, but Aika seemed to have been made with basically the same understanding that he had now. Including the knowledge that there had been other beings here.

Aika was lying in the grass staring up at the sky when she heard footsteps in the woods behind her. Ningen was napping by the shore, so it couldn't have been him. She jumped up quickly as a stranger emerged from the trees. "Hello? Can I help you?"

The stranger smiled softly. "Hi. I was just enjoying your garden. I'm sorry, I didn't mean to scare you."

"No, it's okay," replied Aika. "I just didn't expect to see anyone else here."

"I've been away, but I actually planted this garden. A long time ago now. I'm thrilled with how it's turning out. Are you enjoying it?"

Aika hadn't thought about how this place had come to be and was excited that someone had crafted it. "Are you a gardener?"

"In a way I am, yes," said the stranger.

"I'm sorry, I'm being rude. My name is Aika. I live here with Ningen… he's around here somewhere. What's your name?"

The gardener smiled again. "My name is Hikaru. It's nice to meet you."

Aika didn't know about Hikaru, because Ningen hadn't got around to speaking about him yet. But he seemed nice.

"What brings you here today, Hikaru?"

"I've actually come to see Ningen. How is he?"

Aika had only existed for a short time, but she knew well enough that Ningen was troubled. "He's fine," she replied cautiously.

"But there's something you're worried about?"

"He's preoccupied. He was pleased when I came here, but now he just seems sad."

As Hikaru and Aika spoke in the clearing, something dark was happening to Ningen. He was free, but his mind was still plagued by bad dreams of the Horde and disappointment over Kana. He hadn't heard Hikaru approach, but something stirred deep within him. He awoke suddenly, in a foul, jealous mood, shouting at Aika. "Aika? Where are you? I want you to come here!"

In the clearing, the cries of Ningen were audible, and Aika was shocked and a little frightened. "He's not been like this before," she exclaimed, her heart racing in fear.

"Don't worry," said Hikaru. "It's not him. It's something else *in* him, but that's why I'm here."

And with that, Hikaru disappeared.

Seconds later, he reappeared in the sea before Ningen in his full glory.

"Hikaru! Where have you been?" Ningen was pleased to see Hikaru, but as he stood at the entrance to his cave watching him, shading his eyes from the blazing light, he had a flash of a memory from years before. In his mind's eye, he could see the dream he'd had, the rider who'd spoken about him so kindly. "You're the rider I saw in my dream when I was with Kana!" he shouted, stumbling back into his cave in shock. "How didn't I notice that before?"

"You saw me in a dream a long time ago, yes. But what you saw… it was real."

Ningen was taken aback. "And what do you want with me now?" He screwed up his face, unsure what to make of what he was hearing.

Hikaru glided over the water, drawing closer to Ningen. As he moved, he began to play with lightning in his hands. "Well, I'm here to free you, Ningen. I did it once, and now I'm here to finish the job. You're here in the better place I promised you, but I'm not sure you can quite see it yet."

Ningen was wrestling with a mixture of emotions. What Hikaru was saying felt wonderful, but an angry feeling in his stomach forced him to his knees.

"Ningen? Are you alright?"

Ningen was clearly in pain, and his eyes turned black. He began to creep forward like a hungry animal, like a member of the Horde. As he moved, another being used his mouth to speak to Hikaru. "How did you know we were here, *King of the Eternal Dimension?*"

"Do you think I don't know you, Horde?" Hikaru's face crinkled in a playful smirk.

The Horde continued to speak. "It doesn't matter! We're never going to leave! There's nothing you can say that can unhook us from Ningen!"

The Horde inside Ningen's mind was clinging on tight, and they were right – they would never voluntarily let go.

"I know," said Hikaru. "Which is why I'm going to rip every single last one of you out of him!"

The Horde were furious, but they knew what was coming, and one by one they reluctantly released Ningen and bundled towards Hikaru with angry, vicious screams.

Up by the clearing, Aika could see the most fantastic lightning show taking place in the distance, but the unearthly screams and the sound of unknown creatures snarling and shrieking frightened her to the core. Ningen was down there, and Hikaru said he was going to help, so she gathered her courage and began to race through the fields.

Down by the shore, the Horde ripped and tore through the air, as one by one they were removed from existence. Hikaru swooped through the heavens with all the grace of Seirei. He dealt with the Horde with the devastating might of Kana.

Aika ran, tears pouring down her face as the fear that Ningen might be dying captured her mind. She pushed on, running faster and faster until finally she reached the little cliff over the shore.

As she arrived, the sounds and lights were silenced. In their place came the sound of two men laughing. Aika cautiously leaned over the edge, only to see Hikaru and Ningen hugging and jumping chaotically in a circle like old friends reunited from a lifetime apart. Ningen caught sight of Aika and called for her to come down. "Aika, I'm free!" he shouted. "Come down here. Hikaru brought me to a better place and made me free!"

Aika was quite confused, but still it was a sight that filled her heart to overflowing.

As the evening drew on, Aika and Ningen sat with Hikaru by the shore, eating together, sharing stories, and learning more about him, Seirei and Kana.

Over the following years, Aika and Ningen had many children together, and Kana, Hikaru, and Seirei became deeply involved in their lives. Ningen lived to be a hundred years old, and Aika lived two years more. Many of their children loved Kana, Hikaru and Seirei, but some were still troubled by dreams of the Horde. Thankfully, none of them ever saw or heard anything of Miyako, ever again.

# ACT II

# THE TRIAL
# OF MIYAKO

## CHAPTER SEVENTEEN

# PROLOGUE

Many hundreds of years had passed since the life and times of Ningen and his family. It was a period of real joy and every single day was perfect. Kana, Hikaru and Seirei shared their eternal lives with all Ningen's descendants, and they enjoyed nothing more than spending time in the grasslands with them. Things were exactly how they were always supposed to be.

One beautiful morning, two young people from the community were up early to watch the sunrise and skim stones by the shore with Hikaru. As it happened, this was the very same beach where Ningen had been reunited with Hikaru all those years before.

"You always tell stories about Ningen, Hikaru," said the older teenager as she skimmed a small flat stone across the water.

"What's that, Maddie?" Hikaru couldn't quite hear over the sound of the other child giggling as he splashed a humungous rock into the sea.

"I said, you always tell the children stories about Ningen… but he's a bit boring."

Hikaru laughed. "He's not boring!"

"She's got a point," added the other child before heaving another monster slab into the water. "You do always tell stories about him. I don't know about Maddie, but I'd prefer to learn more about the bad guy."

"Samuel!" Maddie used the kind of tone only a big sister could muster. "You've ruined what I was going to say! *I* want to know about Miyako."

"So, what exactly do you two want to know?" Hikaru said with a shrug and a tease in his voice. "There's really not that much to tell."

Maddie and Samuel could tell Hikaru was messing with them, but they persisted anyway. "There's loads to know!" Maddie said, gesturing wildly to reinforce her point.

"There's so much we don't know," added Samuel. "I heard he had amazing flaming swords and wings as black as the night. Apparently he could teleport, and fly, and—"

"Now, just hang on!" Hikaru bundled Samuel playfully in the sand, pinning him down, and Maddie joined in the fun, heaping sand over his legs to bury him. "This is *my* story to tell. And it's a really good one, so you're going to have to pay close attention. We'll have none of this silly messing around!"

The irony of who was really messing about was priceless, and the kids loved it.

"So… you'll tell us?" said Samuel, laughing, breathless, soaked, and half-buried in the beach.

Hikaru smiled and nodded. "Meet me back here at sunset, and I'll tell you the whole story."

Later that day the three met back on the shore and arranged themselves in a circle around the fire. Maddie and Samuel were restless with excitement as they waited for the story to begin.

Hikaru stood, straightened his coat and then finally cleared his throat. "This," he began, with an over-the-top wave of his arms and a wry smile, "is the tale of Miyako. We begin many years ago, in a mysterious void between the Ice and Stone Dimensions, very close to the end of his life. Not many people have been to the void before, but from what I've been told, those who get trapped there hear voices like echoes through time. Miyako had been there for many years, and he had no idea he was about to have to answer for everything he'd ever... done... wrong."

## CHAPTER EIGHTEEN

# DARKNESS

Miyako was experiencing an eerie feeling of nothingness in the void between the Ice and Stone Dimensions. Time was irrelevant here, so even if a thousand years had passed, he would be completely unaware. This was a good thing, because as it happens, it had.

The void between the Ice and Stone Dimensions wasn't somewhere he'd been aware of before. It was bitterly cold, nothing existed, and everything about it made his skin crawl. It felt like hell; a place of limbo,

where the agony of waiting pounded in his head like a migraine, and he couldn't even move, however desperately he tried.

The void was a place even Kana, Hikaru and Seirei couldn't enter. There wasn't enough air to breathe, and there was no light. The worst part was the silence. It was so deep it terrified him to the core. That was, until he heard a sound that unnerved him even more.

It came from the far distance. Slow, echoing footsteps. If he had to guess, someone was looking for something — or someone.

Out of nowhere, the footsteps were replaced by a chaotic crashing noise, as though someone was ransacking another's home. The noise was still far off, but it was getting closer.

As Miy trembled in fear, he collected all the courage he could muster, and whispered, "Who is it? Who's there?"

The words came out of his mouth in such a pitiful whimper, he felt sure he shouldn't have bothered. But just as he drew another breath to speak again, he cringed back as a loud trumpet blasted in his face, and the crashing noise became the rhythmic galloping of a horse's hooves.

In the next moment, a flash like a raging fire engulfed him, and he was swept up in an intense falling sensation. Before long, he hit the ground with a mighty thud.

The ground felt hard and cold, unlike anything he had experienced before. He began to look around and soon spotted the outline of a tree casting a long shadow into the distance.

He heaved himself up on his knees to study the tree more closely, but froze at the sight of... nothing... in front of him. The long, menacing shadow of a tree was present, but the tree was not. Was he still in the void? It certainly felt like it, but the ground was stone.

"This is the Stone Dimension!" he exclaimed in a panic.

As he scanned the shadowy area, desperately checking for signs of the Horde, the ground beneath him began to tremble and shake. The shadow of the tree loomed strong and stable, but Miyako feared that if this quake continued the ground might rupture and swallow him up.

Of course, as soon as he thought it, it happened, and as the ground ripped open like bread torn in two, so did the sky.

Miyako jumped to his feet and stared intensely up to the rip in the sky. He'd never felt so small, and with the ground still shuddering beneath him he couldn't help but shuffle backwards and then retreat more frantically as fear overwhelmed him.

He came to a skidding halt and stood open-mouthed as rain streamed and lightning burst from a crack of thunder which almost sounded like a scream of pain from the sky.

He started running faster, but before he could get much further, a cloud of smoke and fire billowed down through the sky. He tripped and plunged into a hole which was filling steadily with water.

Now Miyako was completely stuck.

## CHAPTER NINETEEN

# ON TRIAL

Miyako crouched in the darkness. Before him, a crack in the ground was ripping a seam all the way through the land. He couldn't see the whole way along, but the crack tore into the entire field of stone, right up to the clearing where a broken stone slab lay.

He was in no hurry to get out of the hole. Although this wasn't exactly a safe place, it was far better than being on the surface. At least here he could hide away from the firestorm raging above.

Above the hole, the most spectacular event was taking place. It was as if the entire sky was reaching down to grab hold of the ground, and the horse Miyako heard in the void was now also drawing closer.

As the ground continued to shake, it ruptured further and further apart, making it easier for Miyako to inch his way through.

Crawling on the wet, jagged stone was difficult, and the storm made it feel impossible. Still, Miyako preferred this to what happened next. In the time it takes to click your finger, the storm stopped still and was replaced by

the menacing sound of hooves thundering on the stone ground around him.

Miy had no idea what was happening but stopped in his tracks as the roar of the rider beckoned him. "Miyako! It's time for you to come out."

Before Miy could respond, he was transported to the broken slab and standing face to face with a being of shining brilliance. He had wings like pure light and eyes like fire. On his head was a crown of gold and his hands sparked with bolts of lightning. Miyako shielded his eyes and begged for his life.

"Are you Miyako, the *name above all names*?" the rider boomed.

Miyako fell to his knees and bowed down in fear. "I am Miyako, but I'm not the *name above all names*. I thought I was, but that honour belongs to another."

"But you are Miyako, the leader of the Tenshi warriors?"

Miyako replied with his head still bowed, "I am Miyako, but I lead no one anymore."

"You're Miyako…" the rider paused before leaning down to speak softly into his ear, "…the whisperer." As he rose, he spoke again, this time more firmly. "The manipulator."

The rider's words cut at Miy, and he felt the pain of disappointment stir deep down inside him.

"You're Tenshi Miyako, the leader of the Horde, and you killed Hikaru!"

At the mention of Hikaru's name, lightning burst from the rider's hands.

Miyako jumped out of his skin and fell facedown onto the stone, shivering. "The Horde? No! I'm not the leader of the Horde! They're evil and twisted, broken and hungry. They're animals!"

The rider crouched down closer to him. "You're the leader of the Horde, and you trapped Ningen."

"How do you know about that?" Miyako said, trembling.

"I have seen," responded the rider. "I see everything."

"I don't understand. I really don't know what you want."

The rider ignored his protests and paused for some time before slowly speaking into the tense silence again. "You're Tenshi Miyako, and you never understood your own name."

"My name? What has my name got to do with anything?"

This was the right question for Miyako to ask. The right question to move this conversation on, and the rider was pleased to explain. "It means you're amazing; beautiful even. But you're a child of the night."

"What do you mean?" Miyako said, frustrated. "Why are you doing this to me?"

"Miyako, you've carried a shadow within you. It's like a death, except you're so beautiful you attracted the man Ningen to it."

"That's not true, Rider!"

"Miyako, the dark shadow inside you has been here in the Stone Dimension, and it calls to the Horde…" the rider let his words hang for a moment, "…that shadow, that death in you, broke Ningen, and it had to be dealt with by someone who couldn't be broken."

As the rider spoke, Miyako began to worry that he was not going to survive this encounter. "Rider, have you come to take my life?"

"No, Miyako," responded the rider in a softer tone. "Your life has already been lost."

In Miyako's chest, his heart began to beat so hard at this news that he felt sure it couldn't be right. He knew it as confidently as he knew anything. "You're wrong," he snapped back through quivering lips. "I've been here before, and I was fine."

But the rider stood back up and took a step away from him.

"If you're not dead, then why are you in the Stone Prison? Are you sure you weren't also dead last time you were here? What makes you think you ever left? Even now the Horde come here to eat you."

Miy froze in terror. While they were talking, he'd not noticed the Horde surrounding him, drawing ever closer, but now saw that they were indeed close enough to strike.

"Tell me, what do you remember last, Miyako? Before this, and before the void?"

Miyako thought for a moment and then responded, "I remember Hikaru falling from the sky?"

The rider repeated his question. "No. What's the first thing you remember?"

"I've told you," replied Miyako in frustration. "Hikaru was falling from the sky. That's it." His anger agitated the Horde, who were prowling closer and closer to where he knelt.

The rider drew nearer still, forcing the Horde back. "Miyako, I know Hikaru died. I want to know why you're not the leader of the Royal Tenshi Army anymore. I know Hikaru fell; I want you to tell me how *you* fell."

## CHAPTER TWENTY

# YEARS AGO

A warm glow of love and light surrounded the Tenshi warrior's wings as he soared high above Kana's throne. He loved her with all his heart and had the highest respect and admiration for her siblings, Hikaru and Seirei.

When they were alone, Kana, Hikaru and Seirei were incredible, but together they were capable of infinite life, love, sight, power, knowledge, and freedom, which is why the Royal Guard simply referred to them as *The One*.

As he flew, cheers and applause echoed from around the stadium where *The One's* thrones stood. Tenshi circled around and swooped down. He could see Kana, Hikaru and Seirei standing together, leading the applause. They were thrilled for him because today he would take the place of honour as leader of the entire Tenshi army. Today he would be singled out and given a new name. A name that would set him above the other Tenshi.

He glided towards the centre, soaking in the atmosphere until finally he came to a stop above Kana's throne.

Truthfully, he was quite the show-off and, true to form, he landed as slowly as he could, bathing in the adoration radiating from thousands upon thousands of Tenshi warriors. Even Kana, Hikaru and Seirei cheered him.

Every Tenshi in the Eternal Dimension was created to love and serve the siblings, but starting today, this Tenshi would also be served and celebrated as having a name above all the others.

As he drifted to a stop, a feeling of self-importance took him over, and he gazed out across the kingdom. The roar from the crowds faded in his ears, and a strong sense of power swelled within him to the point of overflowing. "I'm going to be served," he said to himself with a secret little smile. "Me, the Tenshi with the greatest of names. The name above all other names!"

Everyone in the Eternal Dimension knew the legend of the *name above all names*. It was said that someone would emerge who would have the greatest of names, and that this 'being' would be praised above all others. The *name above all names* was destined to rule, to be loved, and to be given the highest honour of becoming *King of the Eternal Dimension*. This warrior always assumed the King would be Kana, Hikaru or Seirei, but they didn't seem to want or need more worship. In which case, the *King of the Eternal Dimension* must be someone else.

Why not him?

When he finally landed properly with both feet on the ground, his attention was refocused, and he noticed that Kana had stepped forward; she'd obviously been speaking for some time.

"Your gift of asking questions is the power of pure curiosity, and it brings us so much joy. For this reason, you will be called *Tenshi Miyako*, the first to be named. Miyako, your curiosity is beautiful, you lead well, and we're so proud you're here with us."

Miy soaked in the adulation. He wasn't required to speak, and that was probably for the best. He would have certainly shed a tear.

Hikaru took a step forward. "In honour of this joyous occasion, my sisters and I would like to make another announcement…"

As he spoke, a great hush surged through the crowd.

"Are you sure this is the right time?" whispered Seirei. "Maybe we can wait a little longer before we say anything more."

"As of today," Hikaru continued, "Kana, Seirei and I will be making plans for the grasslands. Plans for a new place for all our people to live."

Miyako stood, holding his new name on his lips. This was a day like no other for him, but something was wrong. A small churn of pain began to twist his stomach.

Hikaru went on. "We're asking for a number of you to join us…"

Miyako felt the shock of pride zap through his chest. Wasn't he important now? Surely this was something Hikaru should run past him first?

"We're asking for a lot of you to come, to set up camp with us. Kana, Seirei and I will gladly take volunteers."

A murmur started rumbling through the Tenshi Army, and Miyako looked on from his new place in his world. There he was, not part of the conversation on the ground, but not part of what Hikaru was talking about, either.

Suddenly, a rush of adrenalin burst through his mind and jolted his body forward. He waved his arms grandly at the crowd. "And I…" he froze, but it was too late, "… will lead any warrior, and will personally welcome them into the Royal Guard."

Miyako knew this kind of outburst was wrong. Not only was it not allowed, but it was also unheard of. At best, the Eternal Dimension was a place of perfection. At the very least, it was a place of utmost respect, but this outburst was born from pure jealousy and humiliated pride.

The entire arena seemed to stiffen as one and stood in stunned silence. Would Kana react? Would Seirei take him to one side and tell him off? Would Hikaru contradict him in front of everyone? No. Of course not.

Miyako stood for what felt like an age, and then, out of nowhere, Hikaru spoke. "Quite right too, Miyako!"

"Phew, that saved the moment." Miyako thought, letting out a small, nervous laugh as the whole army erupted in cheers and applause.

Weeks passed, and Miyako went about his duties, but something had changed. In the past, he knew who he was, what was expected of him and what he could expect from others. Now, though, he was constantly worried about what other warriors thought of him, and he did everything he could to cling to Kana's side.

"Tenshi Miy, do you understand why you have been given this position of honour?"

Kana loved explaining mysteries but was terrible at keeping secrets. Even when she was the one who had a surprise, it was only a matter of time before she told everyone about it. Of course, in the Eternal Dimension, there were no bad secrets, and so everything was just wonderful news.

Miyako looked at her lovingly as they walked. "Honestly, I have no idea," he said with a little laugh. "But I suspect you're about to tell me."

Kana smiled and ran on ahead, shouting back to him as he unfurled his great wings and rose from the ground, flying alongside her.

"You lead, Miy. You always have. You lead the Tenshi into our presence, and when you do, it gives us a glimpse of what it will be like the next time we create something in the grasslands. The next time is going to be so amazing!"

Miyako basked in her compliments, but he had no real idea what she was talking about. What were they going to create? What could be better than him? Still, to be honest, he didn't really care. The praise fed his ego, and the idea of her creating something else pretty much went in one ear and out of the other.

He was her beautiful Tenshi warrior, and this was his time to shine.

# CHAPTER TWENTY ONE

# ACCUSATIONS

"You make it sound like you were treated unfairly, Miyako. Are you really that important?"

"My life with Kana was the happiest I've ever been. I can see that now."

"And yet it wasn't enough, was it? Tell me, Miyako, when did your jealousy turn so sour?"

"It was in the grasslands. I was there, but something happened. I lost myself. It was like something took me over."

The rider wasn't impressed. "You're making excuses, Miyako. Wasn't it simply that you lost control of your rage and used the magic you were given to turn against the ones you swore to protect?"

Miyako clenched his fists and answered through gritted teeth, "I was special. I was the first to be named, but they forgot about me. They turned their backs on me!"

"Okay, so tell me about it." The rider spoke softly. "Tell me how they let you down."

# CHAPTER TWENTY TWO

# GRASSLANDS

The sun was rising, and everything in the grasslands felt brand new. Each long blade of grass was razor-sharp and drenched with perfect droplets of dew.

Seirei flew through the sky and saw the water tumbling over the rocks of the nearby waterfalls. It was as if the mighty torrents had been switched on just for her. As she weaved and glided through the valley, the rivers below filled and life sprung into existence.

Seirei grinned from ear to ear at the beauty, and as she swooped down, she couldn't help but let out a laugh at the sight of Miyako, sprawled out by the largest tree in the fields below. "Miyako!" she called. "Come on. You're going to be late!"

Miyako was disorientated, and only half heard the words shouted from the sky. Late for what? What on earth was he going to miss? He wasn't planning on going anywhere, and anyway, he wasn't ready for an occasion. He was extremely tired. But he was just about conscious enough to respond to his name reverberating through the sky, and despite the state he was in, he could sense the freshness all around him.

He reached out for a handful of lush grass so he could drink the dew from the blades, and then took a moment to scan the area to see whether anyone else was there. Apart from Seirei, he seemed to be alone.

He clambered to his knees and peered over the long grass. It was so dense that the hanging branches of the tree behind him seemed to meet each blade like a handshake from the sky.

Finally, he got to his feet and caught a glimpse of something going on in the clearing at the other end of the fields. He couldn't quite make it out, but could see some flags waving in the breeze. It looked like they were surrounding a large group of Tenshi warriors. As his eyes focused, he realised there were scores of them, and they were all in full ceremonial armour, probably waiting for Seirei.

The warmth of the sun beat down on him in the open field and, despite his aches and pains, he was beginning to feel like this was going to be a good morning. He stayed still to enjoy the breeze on the air for a moment and stretched, allowing the biggest yawn to work its way through his body.

High above, the clouds shone with streams of red and deep shades of orange that wove their way through the sky, painting a dramatic scene. But the power and beauty of the moment was utterly lost on Miy – after all, he was used to seeing such breathtaking skyscapes as he flew through the air. On the ground, however, there were other things for him to marvel at. Out of the corner of his eye, the tree he'd been lying under caught his attention. For a moment, he felt sure he saw it following his movements. Watching him.

The Tree of Magic was something Miy was familiar with. Not because he'd been here before, but because the tree also existed in the Eternal Dimension as well.

# CHAPTER TWENTY THREE

# DARK MAGIC

I n the grasslands, the tree was massive, like a mighty oak. But that's not what it looked like in the Eternal Dimension.

The Tree of Magic served as a doorway to all the other dimensions. So, from the perspective of the Eternal Dimension, the tree was five separate, connecting portals to places where it was sometimes lush and green; or dry, broken and burnt; or frozen and white with freshly fallen snow; or a bodiless shadow; or a blossom-filled triumph of nature.

Just like every other Tenshi warrior, Miy loved to marvel at it, sometimes flying around the top to get a glimpse of life through the various doorways. From the Eternal Dimension, you could travel anywhere, but travelling from the other dimensions was a big problem. Once you were out of the safety zone of the Eternal Dimension, you could easily get yourself stuck, or worse.

Miy often found himself caught up in daydreams. He could be in the middle of a storm and completely miss the effects of the wind. Today was no exception, and he quickly forgot his troubles and dozed off in the grass. As the day rolled on and time passed by, so too did Seirei and the army of Tenshi warriors. Whatever they had been there for, Miy had missed it.

Over the coming days, Miyako made the tree his home. The longer he stayed there, the more bewitched he became by the magic flowing through its roots. Each night he settled down to sleep on the thick mossy ground, and every morning he woke up feeling a closer connection to it.

As he neared the end of the first week, he felt he now knew the tree well. The problem was that now the tree also knew him, and as he slept on the fifth night, a darkness began to rise from its roots and fed his already paranoid mind.

## CHAPTER TWENTY FOUR

# A NEW DAY

M iy awoke with a start after a peaceful night's sleep. He loved sleeping under the tree. The best thing about it was how comfortable it was, but the quiet was easily his second favourite thing. Every day he sat listening to its gentle rustling. Except this morning. Today the silence was broken; interrupted by a mass of commotion in the grasslands.

A sinking sensation overwhelmed him, making him feel sick to his stomach. Was today another important day?

Miyako recalled being told about plans for the grasslands, but he never knew when or how they would be put into place. He just remembered the way it was talked about by Kana, Hikaru and Seirei.

Kana always asked him nicely to do things, and despite how he felt about the tasks he was given he loved to say yes. Hikaru, her brother, was more forthright and expected him to obey, which he didn't like. But their sister Seirei simply made him feel needed. Being important was everything to Miyako.

As he clambered to his feet in the long, swaying grass before his magic tree, he watched as Kana came into focus in the centre of the clearing. She was still a long way off from him, but he saw her immediately, and his heart leaped in his chest at the sight of her. He wasted no time and sprinted over, stopping right in front of her and panting like a hound. He should have felt at least a little embarrassment at not being ready, but in Kana's presence he always completely forgot himself. He edged forward, and Kana embraced him without a second thought.

## CHAPTER TWENTY FIVE

# THREE IN ONE

"I'm so pleased you came, Miyako," said Kana as she snuggled against his chest. "Now, why don't you go and take your position?"

Kana was considerably shorter than Miy, and so when she embraced him, she fit perfectly in his arms. Before he could catch his breath or even begin to enjoy hugging her back, Seirei landed next to him with a mighty thump on the ground. As the aftershock of her landing subsided, her wings tucked themselves gracefully away behind her back, and the Tenshi warriors fell to their knees, overwhelmed by her presence. Kana pulled away from Miy with a smile and he found himself smiling back before catching himself and putting on a serious face. If Seirei was here now, Hikaru must be on his way too.

As soon as Miyako had the thought, Hikaru emerged into the clearing, as tall and proud as Miy himself. "Typical," he tutted under his breath.

Hikaru didn't look impressed and addressed him directly as he circled the clearing. "Where have you been, Miyako? You don't look prepared?"

Miy wasn't keen to be messed with, but he bowed slightly, and in a polite but sarcastic voice, quietly responded, "Oh, you know me, Hikaru. I've been roaming around."

Seirei motioned for him to be quiet and nodded in a way that made it clear he should kneel. But Miy was in a stubborn mood, so instead he slowly walked a few steps away from them, turned, and stood by the warriors in the entrance to the clearing, the tree towering behind him in the distance.

# CHAPTER TWENTY SIX

# MAN

Hikaru began to speak, this time in a more formal tone, and Kana and Seirei moved to stand in formation with him.

Seirei moved first, standing tall at the back, her wings fully outstretched. She took her position and breathed out slowly, billowing huge gusts of mighty wind. Hikaru stood in front, not affected in the slightest by the power of the wind. Instead, he propelled magical words of power towards Kana through the gales. Kana carefully crouched on the ground, her hands outstretched in front

of her. It was as if each gust turned Hikaru's words into a tool of creation in her hands. She simply absorbed both the wind and the words, until finally she knelt on one knee and reached out to touch the dirt beneath her.

Miy stood centre stage to all of this, feeling the full force of the wind, looking Hikaru directly in the face. He always felt nervous when Kana stretched out her hands, and for good reason. With the slightest movement, she could change reality, and he was already not feeling great about being there.

In a moment of pure madness, he took a step forward, but as he moved, Kana closed her eyes and uttered the word that stopped him in his tracks.

"Ningen."

At her word, lumps of dirt and clay before her began to swirl and rise. Hikaru continued to speak, and Seirei manipulated the air even more furiously.

Miy retreated to where he started and brushed himself down. "Would someone like to tell me what's happening?" he muttered as he shielded himself from the dirt being whipped up in his face.

Hikaru addressed Miyako without breaking concentration from the task. "Today, we're completing the grasslands. It's been our plan all along. You should know all about it."

"Completing it how?" Miy asked cautiously.

"The grasslands needs a caretaker. Someone to live here and love the land. Someone like Kana, Seirei and myself."

Miy was incensed. "Like you?"

His outburst was causing commotion throughout the Tenshi army, who didn't dare to look up. No one spoke to Hikaru like that, and no one could ever hope to come between them. Miyako's challenge of them at this moment was highly dangerous. Kana could redirect her power towards him at any second, and if she were to do that now, he would be removed from existence all together. This moment was, after all, a moment of pure creation.

"You misunderstand, Miyako," Hikaru said with a warm smile.

"Yeah? In what way?" Miy said nervously.

"The caretaker can't be *exactly* like us. Nothing can."

"But aren't I like you?" he wailed over the now ferocious power of the wind. He anchored himself to the ground, his feet spread wide, desperately trying to stop himself from falling.

"Yes, Miyako, in a way you all are, but you belong in the Eternal Dimension. The caretaker – who will be named Ningen – will be from here and will live freely here."

And at that, the dirt exploded from the ground in a great thundering shower, and Ningen started growing from the swirling dust. The power of the wind and the blast of earth flung Miyako further backwards, and he screamed with all his might.

## CHAPTER TWENTY SEVEN

# CREATION

As Miyako regained his footing, he shielded his face to stop more dirt getting in his mouth. He watched as Ningen slowly took shape, his paranoid mind convincing him that this creature looked just like *him*. He felt himself losing his temper, and a darkness within started to surface in his rage.

"I can't believe you'd give all of the grasslands to this creature!" He practically spat the words at Hikaru.

Seirei spoke up. "We created you all to love our presence, Miy. Who controls the dimensions isn't important."

Despite the interruptions, the ritual had to continue, and Kana, Hikaru and Seirei chanted in one deafening, defining voice:

"Ningen will live, but only for a time.

"Ningen will see, but only where he stands.

"Ningen will be strong, but only from his body.

"Ningen will love, and will love to create."

As they spoke, the ground shook, and Ningen grew taller, more defined, and more real. Miy couldn't believe what he was witnessing.

The billowing wind, the chanting, and the earth rising from the ground were all creating a frightening amount of noise. Still, they continued without the slightest hesitation.

"Ningen will have the freedom to learn, and the Tree of Magic will be his to look after."

At their words, a shock wave pulsed through the air, forcing the already straining Tenshi warriors to dig their feet further into the ground.

Miy had felt betrayed when he realised that they were giving Ningen the grasslands, but knowing it also included the magic in the tree… this destroyed him. He turned his back on the ritual and stared back at the tree. To him, it didn't matter that the magic wasn't his. He'd felt the pull of it, and he wanted it for himself.

"Miyako!" called Seirei. "Please stop it. You're ruining this."

Knowing what Miyako was thinking, Hikaru spoke again, this time alone and directly to him. "The magic in the tree won't be given to Ningen, but he *will* take care of it." Hikaru was as wise as he was committed to the plan, and he wasn't going to let Miyako get away with spoiling the moment.

He spoke again. "It's time for you to go, Tenshi."

Miyako was furious. "Don't you dare call me that!" He felt belittled once again by Hikaru, and he burst with venom. "I'm not your slave, and I won't be spoken to like this!"

## CHAPTER TWENTY EIGHT

# BETRAYAL

Miyako was supposed to be the leader of the entire Royal Tenshi Army, but he'd neglected his duties to the point of being utterly unprepared for this important ceremony, and now he was out of control. He glared at Hikaru, who had refocused his attention back on the ritual. Ningen was becoming more real by the second.

Now Miy was flooded with a new, grim determination.

His face set in pure defiance, he finally bowed the knee. But not out of respect. He was hatching a plan. He knelt and reached out to touch the shoulder of the warrior beside him. As he made contact, he closed his eyes and used his own magic – the power to question and challenge the mind.

Miyako's ability was limited, but in the Eternal Dimension it was celebrated. His gift for asking questions had always been used to direct the other Tenshi, to lead them and reveal the most wonderful plans from Kana. But now he had a darker purpose.

In a barely audible voice, he hissed his words at the warrior beside him.

"Did Hikaru *actually* want you to kneel?"

And with that, the Tenshi warrior rose, Miy's dark magic bewitching his mind. The power of *doubt* had effortlessly given him control of this Tenshi.

Seirei was taken aback. If this moment hadn't been so critical, she could have easily given the Tenshi warrior back his freedom. With the slightest flick of her wings, the magic-filled wind could undo anything Miyako was capable of. But with all her focus on Ningen, she would have to allow him some ground for now.

"Are you really so intimidated by me that you have to replace me, Seirei?" shouted Miy. "You could have easily given *me* the grasslands."

His words hurt her. She'd done nothing but love Miy for all of his life, but he had never been satisfied with who he was. He was always jealous of their power, even though he knew that who they were couldn't be shared with him.

"These are *my* warriors!" he snarled, rising to his feet with a deeper sense of purpose. "This is *my* right!"

"You've served us well in the Eternal Dimension, but you have no rights here." said Hikaru.

"Warrior, listen to me!" ordered Miyako as he raised himself up off the ground and eyeballed Hikaru. "Draw your weapon!"

Up until now Kana had almost completely stayed quiet, but this was going too far. She reached out her hand and gestured towards Miy. In a flash, his uniform and wings disintegrated, scattering to thin clouds of steam spiralling from his body and his back. He sunk back onto the ground, dressed only in casual clothes as if he were nothing special anymore.

As the lone Tenshi next to him drew his sword, some of the other warriors moved to join him. Others stood up and marched towards Miyako to protect *The Three*.

Suddenly, Kana stamped hard and the earth split, and then every Tenshi warrior disappeared, as if being removed from the grasslands all together. She hadn't gestured or spoken, but she dismissed them in an instant, leaving Miyako without his wings, even more humiliated than ever before.

"I didn't want this!" he screamed, buying some time with a desperate outburst. "Don't do this to me, Kana! Please... I can change!"

Miyako had always just been a member of the Tenshi army, but in his arrogance, he thought he was different. He thought he was better than everyone – a one of a kind – and maybe even the long-awaited *name above all names*.

There was a sadness about him, even when he was in full majestic form. He wanted to be like *The Three*, and he was never content. He was quite powerful, but never understood that his ability was most in tune when he led the Tenshi – in love and service to Kana, Hikaru and Seirei. Now, in his mind, he may as well just be sliding around on his belly like a snake. That's how helpless he felt.

Finally, Ningen was complete, and Seirei stopped moving the wind as Hikaru finished chanting the words of creation.

Kana took a step forward to stand next to Ningen and began to speak quietly. "You're truly beautiful," she breathed, looking directly at Miyako; "but the darkness in you doesn't belong here. You've brought chaos to us, and now Ningen has heard things that were never supposed to be said."

Kana's words pierced him, and her anger burned inside him, further awakening a darkness somewhere in his depths as she raised her voice.

"Have you any idea what that will do to him? It'll break him in two. And before the end, it'll break us as well."

Miy slumped down to his knees. In his mind, he had been betrayed, rejected, and replaced. Reduced to nothing. But he had no idea as to the extent of the problem he'd caused. And now there was nothing to lose.

In that moment, the events of the morning charged through his mind. He was humiliated before them and, as he bowed his head further, rage boiled up through his very soul.

He pushed down through his feet and raised himself a little, his knuckles firmly planted on the ground as if beginning a race. He summoned all his strength and then darted forward; if he was lucky, maybe he could strike Ningen.

In the same moment, Seirei and Hikaru looked at him, then at each other, and knew what he was about to do. In an instant, they both rushed forward. Miyako only managed two quick steps before they reached him and pushed him safely away.

As they tackled him, Kana drew up her hands and steadied her footing ready for action. Miy was angry, and he grappled with Seirei and Hikaru in protest, trying to push them away. He tried again to lunge forward towards Ningen, snarling like a wild animal, but as he fell under their weight, he caught a look of calm on Kana's face that drained the fight right out of him.

Kana saw the event as if in slow motion, and certainly would have had enough time to respond if she'd wanted to. But before Hikaru, Seirei and Miyako hit the ground, Miy disappeared out of the grasslands all together, vanishing into thin air.

## CHAPTER TWENTY NINE

# EVIDENCE

"I suppose you want me to believe everyone's being unfair to you, then?"

The rider was listening to Miyako's story, but in his ears, everything sounded like an excuse.

"Don't twist my words," replied Miyako. "I didn't make myself feel small! I didn't take my own wings away! I didn't ignore and humiliate myself!"

"But you did try and attack Ningen before he was even created? And didn't you just confess that you attacked

Hikaru? Was Kana wrong to punish you for acting in such a way?"

Miyako fell silent.

"And it wasn't the only time you attacked Ningen, was it? Did you not also try to kill Ningen in the desert wilderness?"

Miy shook his head. "No, that's not what happened. I was saving a warrior he trapped. I was doing the right thing! Ningen was acting like a monster. What was I supposed to do?"

"So what, you were teaching Ningen a lesson? Taking the matter into your own hands?"

"That's right," Miyako mumbled, like a naughty child being caught in a lie.

The rider wasn't going to allow the lie. "I can show you what you did, if you like?"

And with that, the events of the desert wilderness played out in the sky before Miyako.

"Look, Hikaru is down there! Drop me now!" screamed Miyako as he whooshed over Hikaru's head.

"Yes, sir!" shouted the Tenshi. And at that, he let him go.

Miyako landed with a roll and stumbled right in front of Ningen, grabbed him and began to shout at him, accusing him and shoving him towards a large hole in the ground. Hikaru tried to intervene, but Miyako was

indignant. He grappled with Ningen and finally pushed him into the hole.

This all looked bad enough for Miyako as he watched with the rider looking on. But then came the moment he was dreading more than any other.

"Hikaru!" huffed Miyako, as if challenging his authority. "The next time we meet, I'm gonna sort Ningen out for good." As he spoke, his breath froze in the air around him, creating an eerie mist. "I'm going to kill him, and then I'm going to make you wish you'd never started any of this."

As Miyako watched, he saw his past self glare at Hikaru and then disappear all together.

"So... you threatened Ningen's life, and you threatened Hikaru as well? Would you like to tell me what happened next?"

Miyako shrugged. "It looks like you can just show me. Why should I bother?"

"Because," said the rider, "it's your story to tell. Come on, Miyako. Tell me how you killed Hikaru."

## CHAPTER THIRTY

# ICE PLAINS

The air was freezing, and light flurries of snow wisped over the surface of the ground. Three years had passed, and constant cold had trapped the tree in a wall of ice that seemed to mark the very edge of the world. The dark clouds dragged on into the distance as if being pumped from the wall itself.

The entire landscape was frozen, and the Tenshi army were camped out as far as the eye could see, waiting for the battle to begin. Although there were thousands of warriors, an eerie silence hung in the camp, broken only by the occasional crunch of someone shuffling on the ice. Some warriors were huddled together for warmth. Some sat half asleep, while others circled around in the sky keeping watch. For the Tenshi, their main concern was being ready for Kana, but every single one knew they would be useless if their wings froze in the cold. They wrapped themselves up tightly and gathered around low-lit fires.

It wasn't until early afternoon that Miyako appeared before the tree, fresh from the events in the desert. The tree looked strange encased in a wall of ice, only the very tip of a branch poking out from it. This was a dimension he hadn't been to before, but if this was the place he appeared, Hikaru and Ningen must be here too, dragging him through time as if they were all connected with a rope. He'd left Ningen down a hole in the desert, so he must still be here, frozen in the ground.

Miyako collected his thoughts. If he was going to stop Hikaru from saving Ningen, it was time to get a handle on what was happening and recruit himself an army.

He looked more closely at the wall of ice enshrouding the Tree of Magic, which was reflecting the landscape in a strange, frosted kind of way. He could just about make out his own face in it. He stared deep into his reflection and, to his amazement, a dark presence stared back at him.

"Who are you?" he said. "What are you doing inside me?"

As he gazed at his reflection, his heart began to race. Something was definitely going on, but the darkness was taking time to respond. "I know you want something!" He glared at his darker self and crashed his fist against the ice mirror with a loud crack.

"What do you want, Miyako?" the reflection said eventually.

"I want to go home," replied Miyako.

"And how are you going to do that?"

Miy hung his head. "I don't really know."

"What if I told you I could give you your wings back? You could do anything you wanted then."

This was music to Miyako's ears. "And what would I have to do to get them?"

"Only what you were going to do anyway," whispered the dark shadow within him. "That's why I've brought you here. Kill Ningen, and I'll give you what you want."

"And what do you want out of it?" asked Miyako, not sure what to make of it all.

"Nothing. I'm inside you, so whatever we do, we do together." And with that, the dark shadow smiled to himself within the wall of ice and then gave Miyako a rush of energy that rushed through him, boosting his confidence.

"For my wings?" Miy shrugged. "I was going to kill Ningen anyway!"

"Then what are you waiting for?" asked the shadow. "Let's get on with it."

The low light of campfires lit up tents across the plains as Miy worked his way down to a tent on the edge of the camp. He squatted down to peek under the canvas and counted five dozing Tenshi warriors inside who were obviously off duty. At the very back, he spied a large bulge where one warrior was leaning, falling off to sleep.

He crawled through to the back of the tent and nudged the warrior, quietly whispering his magic. "Are you sure you're safe in here? You'd better go and check outside the tent. Just to be sure," he said.

Miyako backed out from under the canvas and crouched on the floor, waiting as the sleepy warrior got up and made his way towards him. There was no guarantee his magic would work, and his heart raced as he came face to face with the tall soldier in the light of the fire.

They stood watching one another, and even though it was freezing, a tiny bead of sweat began to roll down Miy's cheek.

And then the Tenshi warrior spoke. "What can I do for you, sir?"

Miyako breathed a massive sigh of relief and took a moment to compose himself. "I need you to clear this area. Pull down this tent, and the ones in front. Then put out the fires and bring me more warriors that are loyal to me!"

"Yes, sir."

The Tenshi army was loyal to Kana, Hikaru and Seirei, but they were always easily manipulated by their old leader. Today, Miyako would make the most of his influence.

## CHAPTER THIRTY ONE

# PLAN OF ATTACK

"Here's how this is going to go," Miy shouted to his troops. "I believe Hikaru is trying to save Ningen. Even now he'll be digging him out of the ice. But Kana can't come here, and we will not allow him to succeed."

Miyako quickened his instructions, in fear that he'd run out of time all together. "You will take down any warrior loyal to Hikaru, and if you see Seirei, you'll need to stop her too." He paused, eyeballing his army. "Do you hear me?"

The legion jumped suddenly to attention. "YES, SIR!" they thundered in unison.

Miyako turned to face the rest of the army, who were now beginning to march towards him. But as he stood firm, about to command the attack, something rumbled in the distance. Was it an earthquake, or just the wind?

The warriors trudging towards Miyako didn't seem phased by the sound, but his heart plummeted to his stomach as they started to raise up from the ground, revealing a cloud of wind and ice hurtling towards him and his group.

They were vastly outnumbered and in grave danger.

"Sir? Sir, we need to move," one of his troops shouted.

"Uh, yeah," he stuttered in shock. But before he could finish what he was trying to say, the full force of the wind and ice broke through his ranks, smashing full on into him and his warriors.

With no wings, Miyako was slammed to the floor, his troops in tatters. Before he could yell for his army to proceed, they took to the sky to fight.

In the next moments, Miyako was only partially aware of what was happening. He knew that against Seirei they didn't have a chance of winning. Still, that wasn't the point. He only needed a distraction to be able to get to Ningen.

Finally, he pulled himself together and scrambled to his feet, still faint and groggy from the blast. He looked around to see his soldiers fighting Seirei's warriors. The scene was chaotic because all the Tenshi were dressed in the same armour, and it was hard to tell who was who. Miyako only had a small number that were loyal to him. Each of his warriors was fighting off large groups of Tenshi on the other side.

The battle had only just begun, but he was surrounded by Tenshi who were wounded and needed help. He grabbed the swords of the injured ones closest to him and raised them up as two warriors laid in to attack

him. The full force of their blades smashed down, knocking him back, but he was a skilled warrior and so launched himself forward, swiping his swords to the left and the right.

Miy was powerful, but against two Tenshi who could fly, he was completely outmatched. The warriors combined against him, swooping in strong from the air. It took all his strength to hold them at bay, but he held on. He would only need to keep them for a second more.

"It's time," the low voice inside him boomed. It was difficult to listen and hold the Tenshi back at the same time, but all of a sudden the dark shadow burst out from within him as if it couldn't be contained any longer. "This is who you are, Miyako, *first to be named*."

The Tenshi bearing down on Miyako were blasted back and gasped in horror at the sight before them. A terrifying creature, bathed in darkness, with wings like a cape at his back.

With a wry smile, Miy flexed and preened, pushing out his chest as he shook his dark wings. He wasted no

time thundering up to the sky, propelling himself hard
and fast before gliding around, basking in the glory of
his new, strong wings, and then shooting down like an
arrow from a bow in front of Hikaru at the other end
of the battlefield.

As he bolted through the air, he cut down warrior after
warrior. One after another, screams rang out from the
surprised faces of his old legion as they tumbled helpless
and terrified from the sky.

The darkness surrounded him and almost seemed to grow with his confidence. He spun and looped around, sweeping soldiers off their feet with a low flying charge that kicked up blades of ice from the ground.

Despite the fun he was having, though, this wasn't at all what he was here to do.

## CHAPTER THIRTY TWO

# SHOCK AND AWE

Miyako was reborn like a dark phoenix, and the shadow within him loved every second, spurred on by his new, powerful energy.

When he landed, though, Miy was surprised to find that Hikaru was doing absolutely nothing to help Ningen, and the fight and bravado faded from him as quickly as the wings of the dark shadow. He was utterly deflated. "You're not digging Ningen out?"

Hikaru was guarding Ningen like an eagle protecting a nest, but Miyako had expected *some* kind of effort to free him. Something to at least prove the love that Hikaru seemed to have for this creature.

"Dig?" said a confused Hikaru. "Is that what you thought I was doing over here? Anyway, where are your Horde, Miyako? How do you expect to kill Ningen without them?"

"I don't want them here!" snapped Miy furiously. "That's not at all what I want."

This was not the conversation either of them expected to be having. Hikaru and Miy were surrounded by war, and these didn't really seem like important things to be discussing.

Hikaru took a step forward towards where Ningen was trapped. "So, now that you're here, what are you going to do? Do you even know?"

If he were honest, Miyako would have to say that he was stumped. He expected to find Ningen being released from the ice already, and he couldn't figure out what Hikaru had been waiting for.

"I might not be able to do anything to you, but the moment you release Ningen, I'll have him, and then it'll be over."

Hikaru smiled at him. "You don't know why you've come here, do you?"

Miyako looked up at the sky, where Seirei was flying back and forth, blasting away at his army. "I'm here to put an end to Ningen. To return us to the way things were in the Eternal Dimension."

Hikaru raised his eyebrows. "And you think you've got the power to do that?"

Miyako shivered, suddenly aware that the sound of the war had faded and the sky was turning strangely silent.

"What are your orders, sir?" a confident voice said from behind Miy.

He froze in terror, waiting for Hikaru to respond, but he said nothing.

"Sir? What do we do now?" the voice said. Miyako dared to look around. To his surprise, he could only see a small group of Tenshi, standing behind him and awaiting instruction in front of what seemed like an empty battlefield. Had Seirei fled and taken her warriors with her? The ground was churned up, and in the distance, Miyako could see his tree had broken free from its ice wall.

But the battle seemed to be over, and Miyako had obviously won!

The only ice that hadn't yet been shattered was that which Ningen was trapped in, where Hikaru stood.

Before Miyako spoke, he checked around.

*Me, the Tenshi, and Hikaru. Even Seirei is gone.*

He checked again. No Kana. No Seirei. Only him, the Tenshi, and Hikaru.

He spun around, cackling out a triumphant laugh.

And then, with a grave look on his face, he redeployed his huge dark wings with a heavy sounding *whoomph* and a stamp to the ground. "Take hold of Hikaru. Do it *now!*"

# CHAPTER THIRTY THREE

# UPPER HAND

Miyako and his minions bound Hikaru and shoved him into the fractured ice. He started to freeze in the dirty water but succumbed to it, as though he was powerless.

"Tell us, Hikaru. How does it work? When you're hurt, does Kana hurt too?"

Hikaru stayed quiet, shivering in the ice.

"You know, I still don't know why you didn't rescue Ningen already." Miy laughed. "Why didn't you dig him out when you had the chance?"

Hikaru looked up but remained silent. Nothing he could say now would be helpful or could change his fate.

Miy spoke again. "Hikaru, if you don't tell me what the plan is, you'll freeze down there... I'll tell you what, why don't you just lay there on the ice while you think it over? Maybe you'll come to your senses!"

For Miyako, this was a new low. In the past, he would never have hurt Hikaru, Kana or Seirei, but this situation with Ningen was driving him crazy. Maybe that was why he hadn't noticed how easily they'd won the battle.

As Hikaru lay half-conscious in the freezing ice, Miyako made his way over to Ningen. "Why are you still here?" He knocked on the ground, as if expecting a trapdoor to open. "Why weren't you dug out yet?" He was completely stumped. "They say they love you... so what are they waiting for? Why leave you here, stuck for so long?"

## CHAPTER THIRTY FOUR

# ALONE

"Hikaru?" whispered Miy. "Hikaru, wake up."

He stood imposingly over Hikaru, who was drifting in and out of consciousness. "Tell me what I need to know, and I'll set you free." He was growing more frustrated by the minute. "Just tell me why all of this is happening, and I'll let you go!"

But Hikaru said nothing, and as afternoon became evening, Miyako was no closer to figuring anything out. For the first time since he woke up in the grasslands, he was indeed out of his depth, but if Hikaru wouldn't speak, then Miy would leave him in the ice to freeze to death. In some ways this seemed perfect. He didn't want Hikaru to free Ningen, so that would be achieved, yet something felt empty. It felt like the feeling you get when something's wrong, but you can't put your finger on it.

Miy took stock for a moment. The warriors surrounding him were quiet, Ningen was still trapped, the Horde were still in the Stone Dimension where they belonged, and Hikaru was alone.

"Alone." Miyako couldn't get the word out of his mind. "Why is Hikaru alone? Where is Seirei? For that matter, where is Kana? Why is Hikaru here alone?"

As he stood between Ningen and Hikaru, the thought continued to eat away at him. Although the area was almost entirely silent, he felt anything but peaceful.

"Alone" He thought to himself. He began to feel agitated, pacing back and forth as Hikaru's life began to drift away.

He turned to face the nearest warrior, grabbing him by the shoulder. "Tell me," he growled, "how did the battle end?"

"How do you mean, sir?" the Tenshi responded nervously.

"Don't *sir* me!" Miyako snapped. "Tell me how you won."

"They outnumbered us, sir, but... but we were determined, and..." the warrior gulped deeply, "...we scared them away."

Miyako smiled at the Tenshi's response, and then a cackle broke from his lips. "You scared them away? Do you know, I was so focused on Ningen I totally forgot." He drew away from the warrior. "It's so stupid. I forgot we weren't supposed to win!"

He broke into a full belly laugh and flung wide his arms, his dark wings stretched wide. "It was supposed to be impossible! It was only a distraction so I could get over here."

As Miyako laughed, the bitter cold of the ice slowed Hikaru's heartbeat to almost nothing.

Miy grabbed the Tenshi by the breastplate and wrenched him from the churned-up ground. "So, tell me again, my very trusted soldier. How did you do it?"

But before the Tenshi could respond, an unexpected, confident female voice rang out from the sky somewhere behind him. "You lost, Miyako."

And at that, every single warrior stood battle-ready as a winged creature thundered past Miyako, tearing through the cold towards where Hikaru lay. It only took a split second for Rhy to see that it was none other than Seirei herself.

He watched, open-mouthed, as she lifted Hikaru from the ice and launched high into the sky with him.

## CHAPTER THIRTY FIVE

# THE END

"The next thing I knew, the entire landscape started to fall apart. It was as if the whole sky was falling. Before I knew it, Hikaru was hurtling towards me. The ground was cracking; even the dimensions were breaking through. It was hot and cold at the same time, and shafts of light split the darkness, but before I could see what would happen next, I was transported away."

"But you know that the fall killed Hikaru?" said the rider.

"I do, yes."

The rider pressed for even more detail, knowing exactly what happened next. "And how do you know that?"

"I saw Hikaru and Ningen one more time. They were here in the Stone Dimension."

"And you used the Horde against them?"

"I did, but that power has gone now. Hikaru took it away. I can't control them anymore. Look." Miyako pointed to himself, crushed. "You can see… I'm powerless!" He knew the conversation was coming to an end but made excuses to try and soften the impact.

"And what did you find out when you met them here?" the rider said.

Miyako knew precisely what the rider wanted to hear. But he didn't want to say that Hikaru was the real *name above all names*. "I can't say it," he muttered under his breath.

"You can't say what?" The rider moved back towards his horse, and the Horde drew around Miy for the first time since their conversation began. "Miyako, you need to tell me what you're holding back. Then we'll be able to move on."

Miyako scrambled to his feet, frustration overcoming his fear. "You really want to know what I remember? I remember Kana, Hikaru and Seirei loving me, and loving how curious I was. They loved to answer my questions, but they didn't treat me like I was as important as I was. As I am! I remember losing my position as leader of the Royal Guard. I remember watching Ningen being created by them, and I remember trapping Ningen for what he did."

"And what else?"

"WHO DO YOU THINK YOU ARE?" screamed Miyako. "I've answered your questions for long enough!"

And with that, the rider turned away to mount his horse, and Miyako reeled as he caught the stink of the rancid breath of the Horde, who were now practically close enough to touch.

"You're not going?" Miyako said, fearing this was the end. "If you promise to stay, I'll tell you everything."

The rider sat still on his horse. "I'm not going anywhere, Miyako."

"I remember Ningen was trapped in the ice, and Hikaru was falling through the sky towards the ground. I looked up to him, and it came to me."

"Go on," the rider said, listening intently.

"*Hikaru*," shouted Miyako. "He's the *name above*

At the mention of Hikaru, the Horde cowered in fear, falling over themselves to back away from the rider and from Miyako.

"And after you realised that, Miy, what do you remember then?"

Up until this moment, Miyako had been confused about the identity of the rider. He didn't look or act like anyone he'd encountered before. But to call him *Miy*... that was so familiar to him.

That was something Hikaru would say.

"Who are you, Rider?"

"I am *The One*. I am Kana. I am Hikaru. I am Seirei."

The rider began to change shape. He had been one being with wings and lightning in his hands, but now the wings were transforming into an explosion of colour; they were Seirei. And the lightning sparked and crackled; it became Kana. Hikaru, the *King of the Eternal Dimension*, sat on a massive white horse.

Miyako dropped to his knees, unable to look at them, as Hikaru continued to speak.

"I am Hikaru. I am the *name above all names*, the *King of the Eternal Dimension*, the key to eternal life, and I've done what needed to be done to free Ningen, forever."

Miy's vision swam back into focus, and he gasped at the shining brilliance of Hikaru on a white horse. Standing beside him was Seirei in all her majesty, nd there was Kana, right in front of Miy, glowing

He bowed lower still, shielding his face from the sight. Kana wasted no time and weaved her hands through the air, summoning the deepest magic. She removed the Horde from all existence, and then walked forward to speak directly to Miy. "You're beautiful, Miyako, but you've carried the shadow of death within you. It's turned you, and the love you felt, into death. Like a magnet, you drew Ningen to you, and he couldn't help himself. That's how he became trapped. But finally, after giving up his life, Hikaru freed Ningen. And then we brought Hikaru back, whilst turning the death inside you inside out. I'm sorry, Miyako, but you're on the other side of death now. It's the end."

"What about Ningen?" asked Miy. "Where's he in all of this?"

"He's now truly free," Seirei said, smiling. "Free from you, and free from the shadow of death that casts darkness over this stone prison."

"You mean the dark shadow in me?"

"Yes, Miy. The shadow in you was always the shadow of the tree," Hikaru said from his horse. "That shadow only exists here, now, with you."

"And Ningen isn't just one anymore." Seirei was brimming with excitement. "Ningen is now many, and they're able to become more with us, and more without us if they choose."

"What do you mean… more?" Miy said, his face darkening with anger. "How long have I been here for?"

Hikaru looked at Kana, and she nodded as if giving approval.

"You've been away for a thousand years, Miyako. I'm afraid that was what needed to happen to allow Ningen to establish and grow. And now it's time for you to go for good."

"Forever?"

Kana leant forward and took hold of his hand. "Miyako, you always missed the point. Just as Hikaru had to die, you have come to an end. If you don't, Ningen will be forever drawn to the death inside you. Hikaru wouldn't be the *name above all names,* and there would be no *King of the Eternal Dimension.*"

"Kana?" said Miyako, as if she were his mother, "I don't understand."

"You don't need to," replied Kana, approaching him one final time.

And with that, she held him as he disappeared from existence.

Forever.

Finally, Kana knelt to touch the ground of stone. In an instant, the hell of the Stone Dimension was rolled away, and *The Three* returned to the light, to be reunited with Ningen's people in the way they always intended.

Living perfectly forever after.

# ACT III

## NAME ABOVE
## ALL NAMES

# CHAPTER THIRTY SIX

# ABOVE ALL NAMES

There's a legend in the Eternal Dimension about a king.

One who will rule all the dimensions, bringing them together into one perfect place for everyone to live. It's said the *King of the Eternal Dimension* will be called the *name above all names*. No one knows where this legend came from, but many have theories and tell stories of ancient magic and wisdom.

Some say the legend was passed through the royal family line to Kana, Hikaru and Seirei. Of course, some think it was all made up and passed around in campfire stories. Still others tell of a far stranger tale.

Some are convinced the story is whispered from the roots of the tree that stands in the centre of the Eternal Dimension. They say that if you kneel next to the tree late at night when all is silent, you can just about make out the words being breathed into the universe like an announcement echoing through time.

"The *name above all names*, the *King of the Eternal Dimension*. The *name above all names*, the *King of the Eternal Dimension*…"

To the warriors who serve Kana, Hikaru and Seirei, the legend is a fun pastime, a spooky story to tell at night around a fire; but Kana and her siblings know the truth. They don't talk about it openly, but the siblings hear the words clearly. Sometimes to them it sounds like a call to action, but often it feels like a warning; like a darkness calling them out, taunting them to war.

# CHAPTER THIRTY SEVEN

# NIGHTMARES

Before the sun rose on the grasslands, a dark presence had begun to sense his own existence at the base of the tree. Life streamed through its roots, but the shadows it cast should have been spaces void of light, shifting where the sun nudged them. Still, some kind of magic had caused this dark presence to spring to life. He wasn't a flesh and blood person, and easily moved through the boundaries of existence, searching through the dimensions in a restless daze.

He could hardly focus on anything as he zipped from the fertile green land of the grasslands into the dry and arid desert wilderness. The transition was a shock. In what seemed like only a moment in time, he'd travelled from dawn to the hottest time of the day. Although he had no body whatsoever, the change was dramatic and unpleasant. Next came the bitter snap of the ice plains in the late afternoon. The cold created a low-lying fog, and the remaining sliver of the sun threw a blue light over the entire glassy landscape. If he'd had the breath to catch, the cold would have half-choked him as he adjusted from the heat.

Next came a feeling of suffocation as he tumbled into the thick, eerie darkness of the Stone Prison, where he stopped dead, barely visible against a backdrop of greys and blacks.

"Shadow. We've been expecting you," came a gruff, animal-like voice from the black nothingness.

"You've been expecting me?"

"Yes, we've been expecting you for quite some time."

The booming voice in the darkness seemed to echo from every angle. A strange, dead stillness hung in the stale air.

"Who are you?" the shadow demanded. "Where am I?"

"You can call us Horde, Shadowman. And you're in the prison of stone. The dead end." The voice in the darkness had barely finished speaking when a snarling frenzy rang out around the shadow, laughing and mocking him for his ignorance.

"And what do you want from me?"

"Find Miyako for us. Find him and then take us back to the Eternal Dimension."

"And I'm supposed to know who that is?" protested the shadow.

"It doesn't matter who he is," replied the Horde. "But if you must know, he's a Royal Guard who's living in the grasslands. We'll send you to him, and he'll lead you from there."

And with that, the shadow was wrenched from the Stone Prison and snatched back through the dimensions. He passed through the ice plains and the desert before rising through the roots of the tree in the grasslands. As the fresh morning air surrounded him he arose, spreading himself out like a dark phoenix flexing its massive wings victoriously.

Beneath the branches and the brush of the tree, Miyako lay fast asleep, utterly unaware of the shadow looming above him.

After a moment, the shadow floated back down to the ground and entered Miyako's mind. He wove himself around the darkness already present in Miyako, and as they became one, Miy stirred and woke up.

## CHAPTER THIRTY EIGHT

# HIKARU

A little earlier that morning on the other side of the grassland, Hikaru sat skimming stones on the lake behind the clearing. It was such a beautiful start to the day, and the water was fresh and clean. Although the sun was already up, a mist still hovered over the waters, and as Hikaru's stones shot over the surface the mist parted, creating little spinning plumes in the air.

From as far back as Hikaru could remember, an excitement followed him around. He was royalty, so some pomp and ceremony was to be expected, but it was more than that; even his sisters treated him with a

higher level of respect. They hung on his every word, bristling with anticipation when he looked like he had something to say.

Maybe it was because he was the first born, or maybe it was to do with his magical gifts. Either way, it often made him feel set apart, and the weight of responsibility played on his mind.

To Hikaru, Kana and Seirei were the real heroes. Kana's magic literally flowed through her fingers, and Seirei could harness magic from the air with her mighty wings. Together they really were a sight to see, and at times Hikaru could forget that what he brought to the relationship was just as important.

Because his words could become actual reality.

When they were younger, Hikaru would speak magical creatures into being just to please his sisters. In his more mischievous moments, he might summon them when they were far away, just to tease them. Kana would roll her eyes and shoot a little bolt of lightning at him for being such an annoying brother. Seirei would also get frustrated, but she could fly right back to where he'd summoned her from. She'd shout, "You're such an annoying boy!" at him from the sky.

Hikaru chuckled to himself, remembering those wonderful times as children. It was so simple back then. "What a shame. We never seem to play like that anymore! Maybe today will change that?"

Today would most certainly be a special day for the siblings. This was the completion of the grasslands, the day when they would appoint a caretaker. A brand new kind of non-magical being. They'd even chosen a name.

*Ningen!* Hikaru imagined what he might be like, what he'd do together with him and his sisters, and he smiled to himself. "This is all going to be really good." He looked around and breathed it all in. "How great is this place!"

Hikaru got up, grabbed his cloak, and set off to make his way to the clearing where Kana was waiting. As he turned to go, a strange, sinking feeling dragged his knees from under him.

He stumbled, nearly fainting at the shock. As he caught his breath, he witnessed something murky rising up in the pool before him. A rancid smell crept through the air, and the grass beneath him withered away, as if dying from the impact.

This was nothing Hikaru had experienced before, but if he had to guess what it was, it would have to be something dark from the tree that existed throughout reality. Despite their power, there was some dark magic beyond even their experience, and Hikaru couldn't help but think they were now under some sort of attack.

He touched the water, creating ripples on the surface, then stirred deeper as he commanded the pool to reveal its secrets. "Show me what's happening. Show me what's gone wrong."

Before him the water churned like a whirlpool, and in the reflection he saw a broken man falling into the desert wilderness. Before him stood Kana, weeping as she disappeared from view. Then he saw the same man hiding in a cave, shivering and crying in the dim light of dying embers in a burnt-out fire. Next came a vision of the man being kicked down into a pit. "This is Ningen!" He wasn't even created yet, but his life was going to be a disaster. "What could possibly have happened?"

Then, as clear as the ground under him, Hikaru saw something that nearly made his blood run cold. It was Miyako. But this wasn't the warrior he knew. There was something oozing out of him like a thick sludge. Some sort of darkness. Some kind of shadow, and he wore the most furious look Hikaru had ever seen.

He scrambled back from the water in shock. There was no time to waste. Kana was close by, and their ceremony was due to begin. Hikaru jumped back up and ran with all his might through the trees. But he was too late. As he peered through the branches and the bushes in front of him, he could see Miyako was already there.

Seirei landed in the clearing with a mighty thump, and now it was Hikaru's turn. He took a deep breath, straightened himself up, and carefully made his way out of the trees. He wanted to jump to action, to question Miyako and to take Kana aside to talk, but the Royal Guard were already in formation, and this was a big moment.

Hikaru circled the clearing and addressed the scruffy looking Tenshi commander who was standing out of formation. "Where have you been, Miyako?"

"Oh, you know me, Hikaru," Miy said with a shrug. "I've been roaming around."

Miy's voice sent a shiver down Hikaru's back, and he looked across to Seirei, but she didn't seem to notice his glare. He did catch Kana's attention, but from the looks of it, nothing was going to put this on hold.

"No matter what happens next, we've got to carry on," he thought.

# CHAPTER THIRTY NINE
# VISIONS

During their ritual to create Ningen, Hikaru observed Miyako doing everything he could to disrupt their plans.

"Miyako, we're completing the grasslands today. It's been our plan all along. You should know all about it."

"Completing it how?" Miy asked cautiously.

"The grasslands needs a caretaker. Someone to live here and love it. Someone like Kana, Seirei and myself."

Miy was incensed and threw a stinging reply back at Hikaru. "Like you?"

"I think you've misunderstood."

"Yeah? In what way—"

"The caretaker can't be exactly like us. Nothing can."

The ritual pressed on, and Hikaru watched things go from bad to worse before his very eyes. True to his vision back at the pool, Miyako was clearly out of control, and Kana wasn't going to allow it to continue. "Have you any idea what your behaviour will do to Ningen?" she raged. "It'll break him in two. And before the end, it'll break us as well."

Hikaru watched Miyako as Kana spoke. He was kneeling, but Hikaru could see that something was boiling within him. He began to shake, as if about to burst with anger.

"Show me what Miyako's going to do," whispered Hikaru as he stood ready for action. In his mind, he was lifted from the scene and watched as if viewing a freeze frame from the side-line. Seirei was gone, Kana was gone, and Ningen lay under Miyako's foot.

"But wait, this isn't just Miy…"

Hikaru could clearly see a darkness creeping from Miyako's body. A shadow, thick as oil, squirming over the landscape. What could possibly have caused such hate in Miyako? "More to the point, where am I in this scene?" He thought.

He scanned the area and saw the terrible truth.

He began to move, walking around the frozen moment to change his perspective. The ground around him was cold as ice. Far up in the clouds he spotted Seirei and, to his horror, something – someone? – seemed to be falling below her. Hikaru took a closer look at Miyako. Was this angry creature with dark wings really what Miy was like on the inside? "Is this what Miy is going to become?"

Suddenly, Hikaru saw something glint behind Ningen on the ground. He moved closer to take a look, but it seemed to disappear from sight. "There it is again," he thought as he edged closer still. There was something there, something in the air, hiding as if behind a veil. He strained forward to see what it could be, and sure enough there was someone there, hiding; almost invisible.

"Kana?" he said, shaken. "Kana, is that you?"

Beneath him, Hikaru felt the ground tremble, and in an instant he was drawn back to the grasslands, dragged right out of the vision and back into reality.

His mind snapped back to the moment, and he knew exactly what he had to do. He wasted no time and rushed forward to tackle Miyako. Thankfully Miy only managed two quick steps before Hikaru reached him and pushed him safely away.

Seirei was with him, and as they tackled Miyako, Kana raised her hands and steadied her footing ready for action. Miy was angry, and he grappled over their shoulders in protest. He tried again to lunge forward towards Ningen, snarling like a wild animal, but he easily fell under their weight.

Kana saw the event unfold clearly, and certainly would have had enough time to respond if she'd wanted to. But before Hikaru, Seirei and Miyako hit the ground, Miy disappeared from the grasslands all together, vanishing into thin air.

As the dust settled, Kana, Hikaru and Seirei composed themselves, trying to make sense of what had just happened.

"Kana, did you send Miy away?" asked Hikaru as he brushed himself down.

"No. Something's happened to him… I think he's been infected by something dark."

"So, where's he gone?" asked Seirei.

"Judging by the state he's in, he'll have gone to the desert wilderness, which is where you're going to have to go too."

Kana twirled her hands in the air, summoning her magic.

"Kana! Wait—" Hikaru began.

But before he could finish, Kana drove Hikaru out of their reality, through the divide between dimensions and into the desert wilderness many years in the future.

## CHAPTER FORTY

# CONFUSION

Moving between dimensions can feel rough, and in her haste, Kana had shoved Hikaru through the barriers with such force it took his breath away. It felt like being propelled through the centre of a waterfall. The pressure was intense, and he couldn't help but gasp as he tried to breathe. The closer he got to the desert, the dryer and more painful it all became. This is going to really hurt, he thought, trying to control his body as he fell.

But there was nothing he could do. He felt himself somersaulting backwards, the sky and the ground flashing before his eyes as he whirled and tumbled before blacking out completely, crashing into the ground by the tree in a great explosion of sand.

He lay unconscious in the wilderness for hours, the dry heat burning his face. Much later in the day, some sort of thud and what felt like an avalanche of sand being kicked over him finally woke him up.

Hikaru sat up, wincing at his aching body, then adjusted his focus and searched the area to see what was happening. "Miyako!" he exclaimed, before tempering the tone of his voice. "You're here!"

But Miy wasn't the only one present.

"Ningen, is that you?" Hikaru slurred through groggy confusion.

Hikaru found himself in a difficult situation. Miyako had already shown what he was capable of in the grasslands, but here was Ningen, scared and alone. "Goodness only knows what he's been through."

Thankfully, Miyako didn't seem to see any advantage to his being there, so took himself off, which gave Hikaru and Ningen time to talk.

As the day drew on, they took a walk together. During the morning, they'd got to know each other a bit, and Ningen had shown him his tree cave, but Hikaru was keen to find out more. They climbed out from under the tree and began to make their way to the other side of the desert. As they walked, Ningen told Hikaru about someone he'd met earlier in the day.

"You know, at first I thought he was dead, but he moved a bit, so I tied him up, and lowered him into a pit."

Ningen didn't describe his prisoner in much detail. Still, Hikaru was worried he might have trapped one of his Royal Guard.

Ningen continued. "I actually quite hurt myself. I limped all the way back to my tree, I was in so much pain, and then when I got back…" he paused, "…there you guys were."

Hikaru sensed that Ningen was straying into details that might end up upsetting him more, so he changed the subject. "Do you remember how you got here? How long has it been?"

"I don't know," said Ningen. "I've just always been here, I think. I do remember there used to be more plants and things, but something must have happened."

Hikaru knew Ningen must have found out how to extract the magic from the tree. The magic was wonderful but would have ruined his relationship with Kana. That's what must have happened.

## CHAPTER FORTY ONE

# LOSING CONTROL

"Ningen, tell me. Does anyone else come here?"

"Like who?"

"I don't know," Hikaru said. "I mean… before today. Did anyone else ever come here?"

Ningen shrugged. "I really don't understand what you mean."

"Well, in your cave, there are a lot of paintings of creatures. I just assumed…"

As Hikaru spoke, he could see Ningen's focus was beginning to wander. And then, as if out of nowhere, Ningen sprang into action and ran on ahead of him.

"Is everything okay?" called Hikaru, puzzled.

It really shouldn't have been a shock, considering the situation they were in. Still, as Hikaru watched Ningen run, he caught sight of Miyako swooping from the sky, and his mouth fell open in disbelief. "What's going on here?" The chaos of the moment threw him, and before he could make sense of any of it Seirei appeared with a thunderous crash to the ground. She looked at him, flexing her wings, and he did the first thing that came to his mind. He called for Kana.

Usually, calling Kana would be the solution to any problem, but calling Kana into the wilderness wasn't working. She would normally respond when he called, but the wilderness was far too broken for her to come anywhere close. He could see her trying to break through, but she was only half visible, as if behind some kind of glass wall. He and Seirei rushed over to her.

"Why can't she appear, Hikaru? What's wrong?"

"Seirei, go and help Ningen," urged Hikaru.

But before she could reach him, Miyako kicked out, sending Ningen plummeting headlong into the pit.

The sound that Kana was making was hardly audible, but cracks and snaps rang out from within what was beginning to look more like a cloud that was holding her presence.

Hikaru looked at Miyako, his face stern. "What have you done?" he demanded, with more than a hint of accusation in his tone.

Miy was incensed. "I've done what needed to be done!"

The cloud pulsed and began to grow larger as they argued. "What do you mean by that?" snapped Hikaru.

Rage boiled inside Miyako, and he flung his answer
at Hikaru with force. "You were supposed to love me!"
Miyako paused and refocused, but he was distracted by
the storm that was starting to rage around the cloud, as
well as the frantic shouts from Seirei.

"Ningen, take my hand! Come on… wake up!"

But Ningen lay helplessly inside the pit, as if trapped
in some sort of trance. "Hikaru, he won't reach for me!"
Seirei sobbed. "Ningen, come on!"

Rain and thunder raged all around them, and Ningen
was fast becoming submerged in the surging water and
sand. Seirei cried out in desperation.

"Seirei, come away!" shouted Hikaru. "This isn't the end for Ningen!"

In the next moment, the cloud flashed and then the ground around them began to harden as the air rapidly cooled. The cloud sparked, and suddenly Ningen was frozen, locked away within his pit as the crackling cloud disappeared, taking Kana back to the Eternal Dimension.

"Hikaru!" huffed Miyako, as if challenging his authority. "The next time we meet, I'm gonna sort Ningen out for good." As he spoke, his breath froze in the air around him, creating an eerie mist. "I'm going to kill him, and then I'm going to make you wish you'd never started any of this."

And with that, Miyako was gone.

The moments that followed the hell of the last few minutes were quiet. Maybe there should have been more activity or panic, but both Hikaru and Seirei were too stunned to do anything.

"What happens now?" said Seirei, panting.

"Now we wait," replied Hikaru, walking towards where Ningen was stuck.

Seirei's heart reached out to Ningen. "Hikaru, can we help him?"

"And then what? He's broken! That's it! If we dig him out like this, he'll be broken forever. No. We need to keep him safe while we wait for the end. Miyako said he would be back, so we'll wait, and when he arrives, we'll be able to sort all of this out for good."

"And then we'll free Ningen?"

"Yes, of course. Now, Seirei, will you please head back to the Eternal Dimension? Speak to Kana, and bring back an army. I think there's a war coming."

So Hikaru stayed on the newly frozen ground to keep watch over Ningen. Seirei flew to raise the army and, as day turned to night, a deep, bitter cold gripped the entire area as the Ice Dimension locked the desert in place, ready for war.

CHAPTER FORTY TWO

# ETERNITY

As Hikaru and Ningen walked in the wilderness earlier that day, Kana was walking in the garden in the Eternal Dimension. Although she was separate from them, she liked to mirror what they did together to stay close and to play along. To Kana, the Eternal Dimension was a place of peace, and that was how she described it to whichever warrior accompanied her each day. This was all very well, but the Tenshi couldn't find much that was peaceful about the situation they were in. Kana never seemed phased by anything, but with

Hikaru and Seirei away, the Royal Guards were unhappy, even to the point of frustration.

As she walked, Kana smiled to herself like a daydreaming child, and didn't even notice her guard for the day approaching her with breathless haste.

"Your Majesty," the Tenshi said, stooping low and waiting for her to respond.

Kana walked on a little, causing the guard to shuffle forward to stay close.

"Highness, may I please speak to you?"

"Yes, of course." Kana ran her hands through the flowers by the path. "Do come and walk with us."

"Far be it for me to question your wisdom, Your Highness, but when might we expect to do something about Hikaru and Seirei?"

Kana smiled and stopped for a moment. "Tenshi, take a look at this flower."

"Of course, Majesty."

"Tell me what you notice about it."

"I don't understand, ma'am. It's small. Does it displease you? Would you like me to remove it?"

Kana giggled and knelt by the flowers. "No, it's perfect. Please don't do that. Just take a closer look."

The warrior removed his helmet and took a closer look at what Kana was pointing out. "It's not yet in flower, Your Majesty. Forgive me, but it's not actually quite a flower yet."

Kana smiled. "Correct."

"I'm sorry, ma'am. I... I asked about what we might do about Hikaru? I have some thoughts."

"Well, that's lovely, but I imagine we might do something about Hikaru when the time is right."

The warrior felt impatience bubbling up inside him but tried hard to be respectful. "And when do you think that might be, Your Majesty?"

"Well…" she smiled, "…it might be when he calls for me."

The Tenshi replaced his helmet and stood ready to be dismissed. "Yes, Majesty," he replied, not feeling as if he'd made any impact on Kana at all.

Kana got up and walked on, then raised her eyebrows in a slightly fake expression of shock. "Would you look at that?" She pointed back toward the flower. "The flower has come into bloom."

The warrior turned back. "Of course," he thought, "she's forced the little flower into bloom with her magic." He stood for a moment, a little embarrassed that she'd managed to suck him in with such a prank. What he didn't notice was that as he looked at the flower, Kana had gone, summoned by Hikaru in the desert wilderness.

The Tenshi stood there, marvelling at the flower she'd brought into bloom. "Thank you, Your Highness. You honour me with your magic."

Silence.

"Ma'am…?" All of a sudden, the guard realised he was alone and ran to sound the alarm. "Quick! Kana's gone! Ready the army. Get in your positions."

This wasn't the first time Kana had been pulled through reality by Hikaru, but whenever she went missing it was the duty of her personal guard to raise the alarm, no matter the day, the time or the situation.

A few minutes later, many Tenshi warriors stood guard where Kana had vanished. By the time she came back, the whole of the Eternal Dimension was ready for orders, and there were many to give.

## CHAPTER FORTY THREE

# SHADOWS

Down in the Stone Prison, the Horde summoned the shadow from the mind of Miyako.

"Shadow. Where have you been?" they growled.

After the hell of the heat, the shadow was in no mood to answer questions. "I've been in the Desert."

"You mean the Broken Dimension?" laughed the Horde.

"I found Miyako," replied the shadow. "But he's crazy. All he wants to do is kill some idiot child man."

"Gooood," snarled the Horde. "Then you're ahead of the plan!"

"Ahead of what plan?"

"If Miyako can kill the man they call Ningen, then we'll be one step closer to being able to leave."

"I don't see how. What's so important about this Ningen? As far as I can tell he's nothing special at all!"

The beasts began to circle the angry shadow where he hovered in the low light of the Stone Dimension. "You're missing the point, Shadowman. If you get to Ningen, Hikaru will follow. He'll come here, and then we'll be able to leave."

The shadow bristled with anger. "You're using me to get to Hikaru?"

"Kill the man, and the barrier between dimensions will crumble!" replied the Horde.

"You will pay for this—" the shadow began, but before he could say anything more, he was wrenched back into the mind of Miyako once again.

## CHAPTER FORTY FOUR

# WAITING

D ay and night seemed the same in the ice plains. The sun rose and set to mark normal days, but it was so low on the horizon that as each day dragged on, deeper snow and ice packed the landscape. The drift was especially bad by the tree, and it was beginning to look more like an ice fortress now.

The journey between the Eternal Dimension and the ice plains was simple, but the warriors hated the trip. Their home was warm and filled with joy, but the place where Ningen was trapped was harsh and difficult. Still, they were ordered to be there, and so there they would be.

Hikaru kept constant watch over Ningen – he never left the Ice Dimension. Instead, he devoted his time to speaking words of love into the ground. Seirei loved his dedication, and she also travelled between the two dimensions as frequently as she could.

"Hikaru, is there anything you need me to do? I'm planning on heading back to Kana for a time."

He thought for a moment, thinking about Ningen and the life he'd once led in the desert. "Have you ever visited his tree? You should. You might understand him better."

Seirei was cold, but she was keen to do anything to make Hikaru happy. "Of course. I'll go now. Is there anything in particular I should be looking out for?"

"Look out for his paintings," suggested Hikaru, smiling as he always did about the things he was passionate about.

Seirei made her way through the camp of warriors. The number was growing by the day, but the space between the clearing and the tree was massive and they still had some time to wait before Miyako would arrive.

Despite the darkness of the ice plains, there was a feeling of hope around Hikaru, but the further Seirei moved away from him, the colder and darker it seemed to get. For the first time, a slight shiver travelled up her spine as she looked up at the majestic tree.

The shape of the landscape was almost entirely untouched. The lip and the climb down remained very much a part of what made the tree what it was.

Below, the cold had hit Ningen's cave just as much as it had gripped the rest of the ice plains, and streams of moonlight still crept through the holes in the ceiling, lighting the floor like a starscape on the ground.

Seirei's feet crunched the ice beneath her, but the sound was dampened in the cave; it was strange and imposing. Ningen had lived a life that had been wasted by the effects of difficulty and pain, and there was something so sad about it all.

First, she saw the painting of Kana; the dancing and the feast, but then she was drawn more to a dark scribble of something that filled the centre of a whole piece of work.

In the extreme cold, parts of the paint had frozen and were peeling off, and this scribble, which had clearly been made all at once, was beginning to come away from the rest of the painting. Seirei drew closer and picked at it, revealing a far more troubling picture underneath. It was a horde of dark, evil, fallen Tenshi warriors.

How had Ningen witnessed fallen Tenshi in his lifetime? The fallen warriors lived in the Stone Dimension and were not allowed out. Still, his painting clearly showed dark Tenshi with features like animals, ripping and snarling at the Royal Guard.

This revelation was shocking. Did the Horde find a way to get into the grasslands? Did they affect Ningen's life? Or was this part of a dream or vision of the future? Either way, Seirei's spirit felt troubled so she left the cave hastily to warn Kana in the Eternal Dimension.

Over the coming days, Kana sent more troops to the ice plains. Miyako would certainly not be long now, and they needed to be ready for anything.

FIGURE ON THE ICE; EYES CLOSED, HAIR FLYING IN THE COLD BREEZE.

"HIKARU, I'M SORRY TO DISTURB YOU. THE WARRIORS ARE COLD, THEY'RE FALLING ASLEEP".

"WE NEED TO HEAD HOME".

MEANWHILE IN THE ETERNAL DIMENSION, THE TENSHI WARRIORS WERE READY TO HEAD OUT, AND SEIREI WAS IMPATIENT TO GET BACK TO HIKARU.

"TENSHI, READY YOURSELVES!"

## CHAPTER FORTY FIVE

# DEDICATION

T he air was freezing, and light flurries of snow wisped over the surface of the ground. Three years had passed, and constant cold had trapped the tree in a wall of ice that seemed to mark the very edge of the world. The dark clouds dragged on into the distance as if being pumped from the wall itself.

The entire landscape was frozen, and the Tenshi army were camped out as far as the eye could see, waiting for the battle to begin. Although there were thousands of warriors, an eerie silence hung in the camp, broken only by the occasional crunch of someone shuffling on the ice. Some warriors were huddled together for warmth. Some sat half asleep, while others circled around in the sky keeping watch. For the Tenshi, their main concern was being ready for Kana, but every single one knew they would be useless if their wings froze in the cold. They wrapped themselves up tightly and gathered around low-lit fires.

At the other end of the ice plains were Seirei and Hikaru. They stood, staring down at the once sandy desert where Ningen lived; the face of that poor creature frozen in the ice below.

"What happens now?" Seirei shivered, her wings wrapped tightly around her chest.

Hikaru knelt for a moment and touched the ice. "There is only one plan today. It's the same as it's ever been. We wait for Miy, and then we set Ningen free."

"I'm sorry we have to do this," replied Seirei.

Hikaru thought back to the time before all of this when they decided to create Ningen. He knew this was the only way to ensure he was genuinely free, but it all felt so complicated. If they did it right, brand new life would start today. But that would also mean Hikaru was going to have to die.

"When Miy comes, you'll leave me here to die. It must happen here to make sure Ningen's broken free."

Hikaru was referring to the deep magic held in his body. He was powerful, but outside of the Eternal Dimension, he was also vulnerable. If he died here, it would release an explosion that would change everything.

Seirei was confused by how things were unfolding. "But Miy says he's coming here to kill Ningen."

"He can think what he likes," said Hikaru, "but he's carrying darkness within him. They have no idea why we're going through all of this, or what's going to happen next."

Seirei opened her wings a little and clasped Hikaru to her. As they stood together, Hikaru wept.

"By the time you need to do it, I'll be ready, Seirei. Then I'll die, Ningen will be set free, and you'll be able to bring me back to life with Kana."

He drew away and looked earnestly at Seirei. "I know you'll want to stay with me, but you'll have to leave. If you stay here, the power from my body won't be released, and Ningen will be alone."

"I don't think I can bear to leave you."

Hikaru was firm. "Seirei, you'll have to. Our lives are linked, and I must be alone at the end. If I'm not, your power will keep me alive, and I won't die."

Seirei knew the plan as well as Hikaru, but still she pleaded with him through the pain. "You'll be completely cut off from us, Hikaru!"

"And that's the point, Seirei. I'm not here to act like the *King of the Eternal Dimension*. I'm not here to rule over this brokenness. I'm here to restore everything. So, I'll die, just as we agreed, and Ningen will be free to experience what life is really supposed to be."

He paused for a moment, gazing around at the camp. "Just look at all of this! The Tenshi know what's happening here, but most of them can't even stay awake!"

"They don't really understand, Hikaru. They don't know how to help us."

As she spoke, Seirei could sense that something had changed in the camp. She watched as warriors in the distance became more active, snuffing out fires to hide what they were doing.

"Hikaru! I think Miy's coming now!"

"Then you need to go," urged Hikaru.

Seirei grabbed her sword, kissed Hikaru on the head and took to the sky.

## CHAPTER FORTY SIX

# THE RECKONING

Hikaru watched as a cosmic battle raged. Warrior fought against warrior, but by far the most disturbing sight was the dark presence careering through the sky.

The creature streaked this way and that, cutting down warriors as he hacked through the air, before crashing to a halt in front of Hikaru. The creature relished his own presence, flexing and strutting to amuse himself.

Hikaru jumped right in and addressed the creature without even looking up. "What are you doing here, Miyako?"

Miy started to explain that he'd come for Ningen but stopped short, letting out a confused exclamation. "You're not digging Ningen out? What have you been doing over here this whole time?"

Hikaru was guarding Ningen like an eagle protecting a nest, but Miyako had expected *some* kind of effort to free him.

"Dig?" said a confused Hikaru, unsure whether he was talking to Miyako or the darkness inside him. "Is that what you thought I was doing over here?"

\*

Back in the Eternal Dimension, Kana stood before Seirei, watching the ice plains with every warrior from the fight.

"Do you think the battle convinced Miyako, Seirei?"

"He was too shocked by Hikaru. I don't think he noticed anything."

"And Miyako's warriors?"

Seirei smiled. "All ours. They're all loyal to us. The only one who actually hurt anyone was Miyako."

"What about Hikaru? Is he okay?"

Seirei's feeling of triumph drained away as reality sunk in. "The Tenshi will do what they need to do, and then I'll—" she stopped short of speaking the heartbreaking truth that she was going to have to leave Hikaru to die, before skirting over it all together, "—I need to get ready to go."

\*

Back on the ice plains, Hikaru was bound by Miyako, pushed into the broken ice. He was freezing to death in the dirty water but was allowing it, as though he was powerless.

"Tell us, Hikaru. How does it work? When you're hurt, does Kana hurt too?"

\*

Seirei was ready; she'd never been more determined in her life. As she took to the sky and made her way to the portal in the tree, there was one thing and one thing only on her mind. *Save Hikaru.*

If only she could!

\*

Down on the ground, Hikaru lay half-conscious in the freezing ice, and Miyako made his way over to Ningen. "Why are you still here, caretaker man?" He knocked on the ground, as if expecting a trapdoor to open. "Why weren't you dug out yet?" He was completely stumped. "They say they love you… so what are they waiting for? Why leave you here, stuck for so long?"

\*

As Seirei left the warmth and the safety of the Eternal Dimension, the air practically cracked around her armour. The temperature was so low she felt the frost hit her wings almost instantly.

Far down below, Hikaru and Miyako were on the ice, but all she could see were thick clouds rushing past her in a frantic sea of white and grey.

She thundered down from the sky, and the ground slowly eased into view. What a horrible sight! The fallen warriors, the broken landscape; it all hurt her heart so much, and she couldn't help but cry as Miyako raged at his army beneath her.

\*

"Tell me how you won!" Miyako demanded.

"They outnumbered us, sir, but… but we were determined, and…" the warrior gulped deeply, "…we scared them away."

Miyako smiled at the Tenshi's response, and then a cackle broke from his lips. "You scared them away? Do you know, I was so focused on Ningen I totally forgot." He drew away from the warrior. "It's so stupid. I forgot that we weren't supposed to win!"

He broke into a full belly laugh and flung wide his arms, his dark wings stretched wide. "It was supposed to be impossible! It was only a distraction so I could get over here."

As Miyako laughed, the bitter cold of the ice slowed Hikaru's heartbeat to almost nothing.

Miy grabbed the Tenshi by the breastplate and wrenched him from the churned-up ground. "So, tell me again, my very trusted soldier. How did you do it?"

But before the Tenshi could respond, Seirei swooped in. "You lost, Miyako."

And at that, every single warrior stood battle ready as Seirei stormed past Miy, tearing through the cold, grabbing Hikaru up and launching high into the sky.

In that moment, only Scher knew for certain that Hikaru was breathing his last. As he faded away, the barriers between the dimensions began to fade as well.

In the distance, over by the tree, the darkness shattered apart, revealing the animal-like claws of the Horde grasping through the air. It was as though the dimensions were colliding together, allowing the Horde to drag themselves out and into the Ice Dimension. It looked as if the air itself was being ripped apart as the reality between the dimensions broke away.

In the sky, Seirei held on tightly to the frozen, lifeless body of Hikaru. She thought back to what Hikaru had told her to do, and his words reverberated in her mind. "You'll need to let me die." But how could she do that? She loved Ningen too, but her every instinct was to take Hikaru away with her. Still, she knew leaving Hikaru was the only way to truly free Ningen, and it broke her heart.

Down on the ground, Miy and the remaining Tenshi froze in absolute terror at the sight and sound of the frenzied Horde crawling and writhing their way towards them. As Hikaru's life drained away, the dimensions splintered completely apart. Bursts of heat and flashes of sun broke through from the Desert Dimension into the now collapsing reality of the ice plains. Darkness swept over the landscape, then light blinded them like the winter sun glaring through the trees. It was utter chaos. Whatever was about to happen was surely the end of them all.

Up in the sky, Seirei ignored everything happening below. She held Hikaru for one last moment, kissed him carefully on the forehead, and then let him go, allowing him to fall headlong towards the ground below.

As he fell, time seemed to slow, and the truth of the day was revealed.

Ningen was stuck, but he was never alone. Hikaru stood by his side the whole time. He watched over him and waited until he could do what needed to be done.

The Horde crashed through the Tenshi warriors towards Miyako, and Hikaru smashed down into the frozen ground where Ningen lay encased, blasting the landscape, the Horde, the tree, and the Ice Dimension apart.

The shock wave from the impact hit Miyako, the Horde, and the remaining Tenshi warriors with such force that it hurled them out of the Ice Dimension altogether. Light, fire, ice, and the most deafening sound raged across the landscape.

The *name above all names* was dead.

## CHAPTER FORTY SEVEN

# PORTALS

Seirei arrived back in the Eternal Dimension, stumbling to a stop and falling into Kana's arms. She gasped, choking through her tears. "He's all alone, Kana. He's gone!"

"I know, but this is the way it has to be. This is how Ningen is made free." Kana gazed directly at her. "It's going to be okay… I promise!"

"But how is he going to come back?" replied Seirei. "Surely he's in the Stone Prison now?"

"I've had a lot of time to think about it. What if we could get to him ourselves?"

"That's impossible!" Seirei said. "Even if I could get there, you couldn't get anywhere close."

"I know," said Kana, "but what if I used my magic to connect myself with you? I could travel as part of you?"

"Okay, that's fine. But how are we going to get there?"

A cheeky smile crept over Kana's face, and she took Seirei by the hand. "We're going to destroy the tree."

The tree existed in every dimension except for the Stone Prison. In the prison, only the shadow sprawled across the landscape; if it were physically there, it would be every bit the portal it was in the Eternal Dimension.

"If we destroy the tree, won't that reset everything we've built? Won't that collapse the dimensions altogether?"

"It's all collapsing, anyway," said Kana. "Look, I've been thinking about it. We hear the words coming from the roots of the tree every night. What if the door to the prison is beneath the tree itself? Maybe we've been hearing echoes through time our whole lives?"

"Are you really willing to rip it down... to risk it all?" Seirei was nervous and found herself having second thoughts about her need to rescue Hikaru. "Shouldn't we wait to see whether he can escape by himself?"

"Seirei, Hikaru's dead. He's trapped. If we want him back, we'll need to go to him. We'll need to bring him home ourselves."

Over the following days, Tenshi warriors began to clear the ground around the roots. The magic in the tree was far too potent for Kana to deal with herself, and Seirei simply didn't have the same skill as Hikaru when it came to making things happen. Still, as the hours passed, they mobilised the entire army and began to heave the tree down. Hundreds of warriors took to the base of the tree with axes, while others tore down leaves and branches. They threw straps around the trunk and wrenched with all their might.

Meanwhile, Kana did all she could to undo every piece of magic attached to the tree. As she worked, she closed each portal, which in turn collapsed the entrances to the dimensions behind them.

In the Eternal Dimension, Seirei was beginning to see the effects of the tree coming down. This tree, which had been standing forever, seemed to be linked in every direction.

"Majesty, you need to come and hear this." A Tenshi warrior beckoned Seirei to follow him and led her to the now broken base of the tree.

"What is it, Tenshi?"

"The warriors are reporting something strange coming from the roots. I think you ought to listen."

Seirei motioned for the warriors to stop what they were doing, and for the first time in nearly three days everyone stood silent.

That is, it would have been silent if it wasn't for the now clearly audible sound of a voice crying out from the ground: "The *name above all names,* the *King of the Eternal Dimension.* The *name above all names,* the *King of the Eternal Dimension*…"

Kana, Hikaru and Seirei had heard the whispers all their lives, but to the warriors it had been a myth. A story they told as they gossiped at night.

"Kana!" shouted Seirei. "Come quick, I think we're getting through."

## CHAPTER FORTY EIGHT

# THE TRUTH

Down in the Stone Prison, Hikaru was locked in a fierce argument with the shadow within Miyako. Hikaru had died in the Ice Dimension, but in the Stone Prison he was trapped and couldn't figure out how he was supposed to leave.

In the Eternal Dimension, Kana and Seirei were working with a renewed sense of purpose. Once all the Tenshi heard the proclamations from the broken roots of the tree, they got straight back to work.

"We're nearly there!" Kana said. "Keep going!" All the warriors around them pushed, heaved, and hacked away at the tree. A new sense of urgency drove them to work even harder.

Suddenly, a deafening crack rang out through the air and the tree finally began to fall. Kana grabbed Seirei's arm and called for all the warriors to back away. "Stand clear! Stay well back, and don't follow us under any circumstances!"

In the next moment the roots of the tree were yanked from the earth, exposing a gaping hole in the ground that released an explosion of light and a trumpet blast into the air.

Kana steadied herself, and then in a sudden blaze of light she merged with her sister, causing Seirei to tremble and sparkle with power. She rose from the ground and began to glide towards the gaping space where the tree had just fallen. Together, they entered the light, and were instantly transported to the prison, where they combined within Hikaru.

Down in the prison, the truth of who Hikaru was burst from inside him like a powerful explosion as he sensed the power of his sisters flowing through him. "I am Hikaru, I am Kana, and *I am* Seirei!"

At his words, the Horde cringed further back, and Hikaru grew in confidence. "I am *The One.* The beginning and the end."

And then it came to Hikaru like a flash – as every fibre of his being reached out for control of the light that was entrapping him. His eyes blazed red like fire, and words like a double-edged sword came shooting from his mouth. "*I am* the key!" he shouted.

The light poured down through all the cracks, illuminating the shadows, bathing Hikaru and finally forming into the shape of Seirei's wings at his back. "I am the key to eternal life."

In his hands, the ultimate power of creation sparked like lightning.

I am *The One*. This is how all of creation will know I am the *King of the Eternal Dimension*. The *name above all names*. I was dead. But now I'm alive. I'm the key to all fullness and all life."

In an instant, Hikaru began to shine like the brightest sun, banishing Miyako into nothingness with the force of the light. As the moment pressed on, the Horde scattered, completely disorientated, and before they could compose themselves, Hikaru and Ningen were gone.

## CHAPTER FORTY NINE

# REUNITED

"Is he awake?"

"Let him sleep, Seirei, he's been through a lot," said Kana.

Seirei leant down, a mischievous smile playing on her lips, and whispered in Hikaru's ear, "I'm going to splash you with water. If you don't want me to, you'd better wake up."

Kana giggled, trying hard to stay quiet. "No! Stop it, he'll be cross!"

"He won't be." Seirei laughed as she ruffled Hikaru's hair. "Because he's asleeeeep!"

"Can't you girls leave me alone for just a minute?" Hikaru was awake, but too stiff to move; he ached all over. He was tired, but that didn't stop the pleasure he felt at hearing his sisters' voices. An easy smile crept over his face. "You're both so annoying!"

"What's that, Hikaru?" Kana said with more than a hint of playful sarcasm. "Did you just admit that you're annoying?"

Hikaru scowled for a moment, and then all three of them burst into fits of laughter.

Hikaru's eyes were still adjusting to the light, but he couldn't help but notice they were in a lush garden, by a pool that looked so much like the grasslands. "Where are we, Kana?"

"It's called Joy," replied Kana, her face lit with a big grin.

"It's not called Joy!" Seirei slapped her hand to her forehead. "You're such a child!"

"Well, it makes me happy. It's the only dimension left, and that's what I'm going to call it."

Hikaru looked at her. "Seriously, though—"

"Seriously? If you want me to be serious, we should probably call it *'Kana-land'.*"

Hikaru let out a little chuckle. "I can see I'm not going to get any helpful information from either of you right now, am I?"

Seirei laid her hand on Hikaru's cheek and smiled with a warmth so welcome after everything they'd been through. "I think we've had enough of serious for a lifetime, don't you?"

They all laughed.

"So, what's happening now?" Hikaru said.

Kana smiled. "Do you want the good news or the bad news?"

"The good," said Hikaru, throwing his head back and rolling his eyes. "Please just the good."

"You get to meet someone new today!"

"Someone new?"

"Yes," said Kana. "Head over to the clearing and you'll see. Her name's Aika."

"And Ningen? Is he the bad news?"

"Unfortunately, yes," said Seirei. "But don't worry too much. He just needs a friend to show him this is a better place."

"Again? Am I going alone, or are we going together?"

"Oh!" Kana grinned widely. "I wouldn't miss this. We're definitely going together."

And they did.

From then on, Kana, Hikaru and Seirei were hardly ever apart. Sometimes they joined forces when they needed to confront a difficult situation, but at other times they separated to play and to do things that interested them alone. When they combined their power, the Tenshi described them as *The One*, but that was mostly when they told stories of how they saved Ningen.

In the following years, the siblings established their home with Ningen and his people. He and his wife, Aika, were famous, and even when they had passed on, Hikaru continued to tell their story. He told of how Ningen got lost, how Miyako had attacked him, and how he, Kana and Seirei beat the dark shadow of death once and for all.

## CHAPTER FIFTY

# YEARS LATER

The sun had risen already; it was a new day in the grasslands. As Seirei soared overhead, she could see the water tumbling down the rocks in the nearby falls. As the flowing rivers weaved through the valley, so did Seirei. She grinned from ear to ear at the beauty, and as she swooped down, she couldn't help but marvel at the sight of everyone enjoying this joyful new Light Dimension.

Kana laughed and played with the children under the beautiful hanging branches of the new tree, and Hikaru sat in the clearing at the other end of the fields with their parents, teaching them and telling them stories.

"Can we go and listen, Seirei?" called the very eager child who was hitching a ride on her back.

"Are you sure?" Seirei shouted back, with a wry smile. "Hikaru goes on and on and on!" As she repeated the joke, she circled round and round in the most delightful, playful manner, sending the child into crazy whoops of excitement.

"Yes, I love his stories!" the child shouted, pulling at Seirei's hair, trying to direct her. "Pleeease can we go?"

Seirei loved to tease, so pretended to be unhappy about it, but then rose to hover in the sky before shouting, "Okay, hang on!" and then swooping down fast like an eagle.

As she soared down, the child clung on tightly, screaming with joy before they came in gracefully to land.

"And it was right here that you were first brought into being," recounted Hikaru, without breaking his flow,

"and it was on this very same spot Ningen was released from Miyako's trap."

"Is this also where you died?" asked one of the parents.

"Yes, that's right. This is also the place Aika sprang to life from the power of my death."

As Hikaru continued to speak, the child clambered down from Seirei's back and ran straight over to Hikaru, weaving through the grown-ups and mimicking Seirei's flight through the sky. "And where is Miy now?" she shouted, interrupting the conversation.

"Well." Hikaru smiled as the child jumped onto his lap. "Miy has no power now, and so he's not able to be in the fields with us."

"My daddy says that sometimes I'm very naughty like him," the child replied with an embarrassed smile.

"Yes, I'm sure you are," laughed Hikaru, hugging the very wriggly child, who then shuffled out of his grip, jumped down, and started singing. "But it's okay to be naughty!"

The whole crowd burst into fits of laughter, and her father raced forward and scooped her up. "No, it's not okay to be naughty!" he said, laughing and swinging her around in his arms before setting her down, at which point she immediately pranced off to find Kana, singing and dancing the whole way.

As the day went on, Kana, Hikaru and Seirei shared themselves with all the people in the grasslands, and as the day drew to an end, they gathered around the clearing where a raging fire provided heat and light for everyone there. The day was perfect, and they had enjoyed each other's company, considering each other as equals. Many parts, but together, they were simply one.

The little girl sat half asleep in Hikaru's arms, listening to the crackling embers of the fire as her parents sang, and her siblings laughed and played with their friends.

"Tell me the story of Ningen, Hikaru," she whispered, drifting in and out of sleep.

Hikaru smiled and looked around at everyone having fun around him. "I'll do one better, Evelyn. In the morning, we'll all go down to the sea. We'll visit his cave, and I'll tell you his story right there on the shore."

And as the evening turned to night, the little girl fell fast asleep.

# ACT IV

## HIKARU
## EXPLAINED

### A LETTER FROM THE AUTHOR

# HUNGRY?

I love to cook. One day I'm cooking for my family, and my kids are in the next room playing on their games console. It's a familiar scene in our house; probably the same in yours.

"Guys, can you set the table, please?" I call from the kitchen.

Of course, there's no response.

"Hey! I need the table laid!" I shout, my voice taking on a frustrated, gruff tone.

Ten or so minutes pass, and I'm still cooking. The table's still unlaid, and the kids are fighting, or building, or driving on their game. But then an amazing, mystical thing happens.

As the food I'm cooking begins to get hot, tiny particles jump out and surf the steam all the way out of the kitchen and into the living room. Without my kids having any idea why, they start to feel hungry.

The tiny particles have made it all the way to the other side of the living room, and my son has a thought and shouts through to me in the kitchen, "Daddy! What's for dinner?"

He has no idea that I'd called for them to set the table ten minutes ago, and he has no idea that his brain has been infiltrated by the smell of the food. But now, and only now, he's completely ready to listen.

"Hey, mate," I calmly respond, "it's pizza. Would you like to set the table?"

And, of course, now he's feeling hungry, the table gets laid in two minutes flat: he sets out flowers, candles, the best cutlery, bone china, a beautiful tablecloth, and somehow, he's also got completely changed into his best clothes and soon he's sitting up ready to eat with a napkin tucked into his collar like a bib.

Why are we talking about dinner?

Have you ever had anyone try to tell you about Jesus, or try to explain the Trinity? Maybe you've even had someone try to help you understand sin and death and why Jesus had to die, only to be left feeling like your brain checked out before you even arrived.

Honestly, until you're ready, until you're hungry, you may not even be capable of understanding about Jesus. Just as my son wasn't able to hear it was dinner time until he was hungry, you won't be passionate about Jesus until you sense God for yourself.

And if this is true, then you might need to chill out about it.

So, you don't fully *get* Jesus yet? It's fine. I don't get it all either. But I do want to, and so I ask God to reveal what I need to know as I read the Bible and listen to the people who are trying to teach me.

Now, what's all of this got to do with this book you're holding? You might not have realised, but you've just read a lot of important things about Jesus and our relationship with Him in a fictional story.

In the following five mini chapters, you're going to read about who all the main characters are, and what they've got to do with Jesus and you.

# WHO IS HIKARU?

There are so many things about Jesus that are hard to get your head around. Is He God himself? Is He God's son? Was He there when God created the world? Did He sing in the shower?

These are all excellent questions, but to find out who Jesus is, you need to read the gospel of John:

> ### JOHN 1: 1-5 (NLT)
>
> IN THE BEGINNING, THE WORD ALREADY EXISTED.
> THE WORD WAS WITH GOD,
> AND THE WORD WAS GOD.
> HE EXISTED AT THE BEGINNING WITH GOD.
> GOD CREATED EVERYTHING THROUGH HIM,
> AND NOTHING WAS CREATED EXCEPT THROUGH HIM.
> THE WORD GAVE LIFE TO EVERYTHING THAT WAS CREATED,
> AND HIS LIFE BROUGHT LIGHT TO EVERYONE.
> THE LIGHT SHINES IN THE DARKNESS,
> AND THE DARKNESS CAN NEVER EXTINGUISH IT.

Let's figure this out for a second. Did you notice it was Hikaru's words that were his power? Well, that's because the best way to think about Jesus is as the Word of God. That's what the gospel of John is saying.

Imagine that you're a superhero. That's right, you're a superhero, and you fight crime. But forget flying or being invisible; your superpower is that when you speak, the words you say turn into a person who can fight crime with you. That's right – your words are so filled with power they can live as another you.

You see, when Jesus was a man, he never stopped being God. He was God's actual words on a mission. A mission to save Ningen. To save us!

He was there as God's Word when He created the world and the universe. He was there as God's Word when he was made into a real, flesh-and-blood man. And He still exists now as the Word of God.

# WHO IS NINGEN?

When I was younger, I'd heard about Jesus healing people, and I'd heard about Him being tempted in the desert, but I'd probably heard about His love more than anything. His love for us.

In the story, it's Kana, Hikaru and Seirei who come together to make Ningen. They give him gifts of love, sight, strength, and freedom. This doesn't exactly happen in the Bible, but in a way it does.

At the very beginning of the Bible, it says this:

You see, God exists forever. God is love. God sees everything. God is power. God knows everything. And God is freedom. So, when he says He's going to make us like Him, it's safe to say that we have the same gifts. Just smaller, human versions.

You know, like words, except our words aren't powerful enough to grow legs and fight crime with us. Our words can still be powerful though, can't they?

So, there's love, sight, strength, and freedom, but there's also knowledge, and this is where our problems begin.

In the story, Miyako was worried Ningen would take the magic from the tree, and Kana warned Ningen about it too. Well, at the beginning of the Bible, God specifically tells us not to take from the tree of knowledge, but when we disobeyed God, everything went wrong. You see, God wasn't acting in an unhelpful way. The truth is that when we resisted Him, we became broken in a way that we could never fix on our own.

Like Ningen, we became capable of saying the wrong things, doing the wrong things and even ruining the world around us. In some ways, we also act like Miyako, trying to get our way all the time. Maybe you've even acted like that today?

Remember what we were talking about before? Jesus is God walking around as a man, and that's why we read about Him teaching, healing and providing for people. If you put a good person where there is a need, they'll respond. Imagine what putting God on Earth could accomplish!

# WHO IS KANA?

There was this one day, when my elder brother and I went to the supermarket for our mum. We had her list, which was pretty standard. You know the sort of thing: toilet roll, bread, milk, crisps, washing up liquid, and baking powder. But alongside her list, we had a secret one of our own. She'd given us money for her list, but our list was made up of sweets that we were going to steal.

We got everything Mum wanted, and we got away with stealing what we wanted, too – that is until we got home.

You see, the shop didn't know we'd stolen, but our mum knew instinctively that we'd done something wrong the moment we walked through the door. She just seemed to be able to sense our guilt, and we were in big trouble.

To be honest, now that I'm a dad, I understand a bit more about how my mum knew we'd done something wrong, and now our kids think that we've got superpowers in the same way I thought my parents did. But the truth is, no one actually has superpowers; it's just that the older you get, the more you see and understand.

This is also true of Kana. In this story, I like to think of Kana as the part of God we typically call Father. As in the *Our Father, who art in heaven* part of God.

You remember me saying about how massive God is, and how we're made in His image with smaller, human versions of what makes God, God? Well, that's the same here too.

As hard as it might sound, I don't always fully understand why Jesus had to die to save us, but God, the Father, is way bigger and older than I can imagine, and so like with my mum, I have to accept there are things just too big for me to understand.

Here's something I do understand, though. For something to be properly fixed, something that isn't broken or that can't be broken in the same way has to sort it out.

That's what Kana said in the story, and that's why Hikaru had to die. Because although He would die, Kana and Seirei would raise Him back from the dead again.

Ningen gets trapped, and Hikaru gives up his life to set him free, which is exactly the same way that Jesus set *us* free. If you take a look in the book of Romans, you'll find that Paul says this:

> **ROMANS 5:10 (NLT)**
>
> FOR SINCE OUR FRIENDSHIP WITH GOD WAS RESTORED BY THE DEATH OF HIS SON (JESUS) WHILE WE WERE STILL HIS ENEMIES, WE WILL CERTAINLY BE SAVED THROUGH THE LIFE OF HIS SON (JESUS).

And that's it right there. When we were broken, we were enemies of God, but that's not what God wanted. And so, through God's own death, we've been set free, ready for an eternity lived because of the power of Jesus.

# WHO IS MIYAKO?

Have you ever noticed how the thing that's bad for you is always the thing you want the most?

Your appetite can get so out of control that you can be sure it wants to explode your stomach with chocolate, pizza, and chips, topped off with fizzy drinks, ice cream, and a bacon sandwich.

Your need for cool things is so excitable that if left unchecked, you'd undoubtedly be swimming in your own personal pile of amazing battery-operated cars, quadcopters, and hover-boards.

And your love for attention or being seen is so hungry you could be rejected for just a second by the wrong person and it could ruin your entire day, sending you into another bowl of ice cream and Minstrels.

Does that sound familiar?

This is exactly what I mean! Things that are bad for us try to do us in! Where do you think the phrase 'misery loves company' comes from?

That is, except these very same things can also be amazing; even beautiful. Of course, there's absolutely nothing wrong with any of these things, except that without discipline or a good understanding of what is actually good for us, we could quickly become obsessed and even make them more important than the good things in our lives.

And that's who Miyako is. He's our unchecked crazy *needs* that seek to bury us in stuff and nonsense. He's the lie that we need more of anything to be happy. He's the whisper that always tells us Jesus isn't worth the effort. Except I know He is. Jesus paid the ultimate price in dying for us to save us from everything we've done wrong and everything that traps us, separating us from His love.

In the story, you know Miyako was the bad guy, but it's too easy to think of him as Satan, the ultimate enemy of life. He's tricky, and so likeable that at times it almost felt as if he was writing himself to be the good guy. There were even times I liked him so much that I wanted him to win.

Here's a question for you. Were you ever tempted by Miyako in the story? Did he convince you of anything?

Whatever you thought of him, the most essential thing in this entire story was about how God made you and is so pleased with you.

God knew that your needs would overtake you, and so before you were born, He planned to die so you could know real fullness and freedom, the kind that lasts.

Jesus came into our world to become like us. He spent time with us, telling us about the kingdom of heaven, healing people and showing us love while we ignored and rejected Him.

He died a criminal's death on a cross, but in doing that He turned death inside out.

And now He lives again, the King over all creation, and His name has been placed above all other names so that you can live forever with Him, discovering more every day about what life is like when it's lived for Him.

### PHILIPPIANS 2: 6-11 (NLT)

THOUGH HE WAS GOD, HE DID NOT THINK OF EQUALITY WITH GOD AS SOMETHING TO CLING TO. INSTEAD, HE GAVE UP HIS DIVINE PRIVILEGES; HE TOOK THE HUMBLE POSITION OF A SLAVE AND WAS BORN AS A HUMAN BEING.

WHEN HE APPEARED IN HUMAN FORM, HE HUMBLED HIMSELF IN OBEDIENCE TO GOD AND DIED A CRIMINAL'S DEATH ON A CROSS.

THEREFORE, GOD ELEVATED HIM TO THE PLACE OF HIGHEST HONOUR AND GAVE HIM THE NAME ABOVE ALL OTHER NAMES, THAT AT THE NAME OF JESUS EVERY KNEE SHOULD BOW, IN HEAVEN AND ON EARTH AND UNDER THE EARTH, AND EVERY TONGUE DECLARE THAT JESUS CHRIST IS LORD, TO THE GLORY OF GOD THE FATHER.

You're a child of God. You're loved and you've been set free to know Him, bought at a great price to escape eternal death. And all of this is made possible by the overwhelming, crazy love of a good God who has chased you through reality to call you His very own.

And if you don't understand it all, that's okay, but I hope your heart has been stirred to know more about Jesus as we've gone through this together.

If it has, you might want to go and tell someone who already knows Jesus for themselves. Go and tell someone and ask them if they'll tell you more.

# WHO IS SEIREI?

One of the hardest things about understanding Jesus, is that we say *He came back from death* as proof that He fixed everything wrong with us and the world, but if you look around, you can see for yourself things aren't actually perfect right now.

He was there to make us, to save us, to come back from death to have a friendship with us, but it's almost as if the plan didn't really work.

You see, although the world around us isn't perfect right now, with Seirei in our lives it doesn't have to be. I mean, it will be one day when God sorts it out, but for now, Seirei can show you who God is and how He can transform your life as you live every day.

I keep saying Seirei, but of course I mean to say that I wrote Seirei to be similar to the Holy Spirit. The part of God that can be with us every single moment of every day. In the Bible, when Jesus comes back from death, He promises the Holy Spirit will be with us in every situation, for our entire lives:

**JOHN 14:15-17 (NLT)**

IF YOU LOVE ME, OBEY MY COMMANDMENTS. AND I WILL ASK THE FATHER, AND HE WILL GIVE YOU ANOTHER ADVOCATE, WHO WILL NEVER LEAVE YOU. HE IS THE HOLY SPIRIT, WHO LEADS INTO ALL TRUTH.

In our story, Seirei is the wind. She's powerful, playful, excitable and above all, she loves to soar high in the sky. And the Holy Spirit is similar, but also so much more.

If you're struggling, sad, happy, excited, or full of dread about something, the Holy Spirit is there to be with you, to point you to Jesus and to help you experience an amazing life lived for God, from the moment you invite Him into your life, and even before that!

I'll never forget when I invited God to transform my life. Actually, to be honest, I invited God to be a part of my life about ten times. I wasn't sure whether I asked Him right. Of course, you can't actually ask Him wrongly, but I wasn't sure, and so one night I made absolutely certain that I did it right.

It was a spring night in 1993 when I was visiting a church with my friend to watch a play that had a Christian message. After the play finished a guy stood up to tell us about Jesus. He was really funny and what he was saying struck me.

He said that he wished he could introduce us to God. He said something like this:

"Wouldn't it be amazing if I could introduce God to you? I'd say, 'Ladies and Gentlemen, please welcome God!' and then God would crash through the roof with angels dressed in nighties, and trumpets would sound, and everyone would be shocked and excited and then we'd all know that God was real. Except if God did that, you'd go home and tell your parents, and they definitely wouldn't believe you. They'd say that you imagined it, or that it was a trick. And then you'd probably think it was a trick and stop believing. Which is why God doesn't work like that!"

The guy went on for a bit longer and explained some more but then came to the main point.

"The truth is that although God won't smash the actual ceiling in, He will crash through the ceiling of your heart. And if you want Him to, He'll change you from the inside out, transforming you so you can live for Him."

As he came to an end, he explained that accepting Jesus won't make everything easy or perfect. But he told me something that has stayed with me ever since.

"A life lived with God won't be easy, but it'll be filled with the freedom that comes from the God who made you, who lived and died for you. Then rose from death for you, and who is now available to live in your heart every single day through the Holy Spirit."